RANDOM
HOUSE
LARGE
PRINT

the water cure

the water cure

A NOVEL

Sophie Mackintosh

This is a work of fiction. Names, characters, places, and incidents either are the product of the author's imagination or are used fictitiously. Any resemblance to actual persons, living or dead, events, or locales is entirely coincidental.

Published in the United States of America by Random House Large Print in association with Doubleday, a division of Penguin Random House LLC, New York.
Originally published in Great Britain by Hamish Hamilton, an imprint of Penguin Books Ltd., a division of Penguin Random House Ltd., London, in 2018.

Cover design by Michael J. Windsor
Cover photograph © Johanna Negowski

The Library of Congress has established a Cataloging-in-Publication record for this title.

ISBN: 978-0-593-10421-7

www.penguinrandomhouse.com/large-print-format-books

FIRST LARGE PRINT EDITION

Printed in the United States of America

10 9 8 7 6 5 4 3 2 1

This Large Print edition published in accord with the standards of the N.A.V.H.

For Annys and Beverley, my sisters

contents

part one

father

grace, lia, sky

ONCE WE HAD a father, but our father dies without us noticing.

It's wrong to say that we don't notice. We are just absorbed in ourselves, that afternoon when he dies. Unseasonable heat. We squabble, as usual. Mother comes out on the terrace and puts a stop to it by raising her hand, a swift motion against the sky. Then we spend some time lying down with lengths of muslin over our faces, trying not to scream, and so he dies with none of us women bearing witness, none of us accompanying him.

It is possible we drove him away, that the energy escaped our bodies despite our attempts to stifle it and became a smog clinging around the house, the forest, the beach. That was where we last saw him. He put a towel on the ground and lay down parallel to the sea, flat on the sand. He was resting, letting sweat gather along his top lip, his bare head.

The interrogation begins at dinner when he fails to turn up. Mother pushes the food and plates from the table in her agitation, one sweep of the arm, and we search the endless rooms of the house. He is not in the kitchen, soaking fish in a tub of brine, or pulling up withered potatoes outside, inspecting the soil. He is not on the terrace at the top of the house, surveying the still surface of the pool three floors below, and he is certainly not in the pool itself, for the sound of his splashing is always violent enough to carry. He is not in the lounge, nor the ballroom, the piano untouched, the velvet curtains heavy with undisturbed dust. Moving up the staircase again, a spine through the centre of the house, we check our rooms individually, our bathrooms, though we know he will not be there. From our scattered formation we come together to search the garden, search deeper, sticking long branches into the pond's green murk. Eventually we are out on the beach and we realize one of the boats has gone too—a furrow in the sand where it has been pushed out.

5

For a moment we think he has gone for supplies, but then we remember he was not wearing the protective white suit, we did not do the leaving ceremony, and we look towards the rounded glow of the horizon, the air peach-ripe with toxicity. And Mother falls to her knees.

Our father had a big and difficult body. When he sat down, his swimming shorts rode up and exposed the whiteness of his thigh where it was usually covered. If you killed him, it would be like pushing over a sack of meat. It would require someone much stronger than us.

The father shape he leaves behind quickly becomes a hollow that we can put our grief into, which is an improvement in a way.

grace

I ASK MOTHER if she had noticed any sickness in you. Any hint of your body giving way. She says, "No, your father was in fine fettle." Dark turn. "As you well fucking know."

Your body was not completely all right. Of course I would see that where she would not. I noticed a slight cough, mixed up a honey tincture for you the day before you died. Boiled nettles from the end of the garden, where we dump our rubbish and leave things to rot. My hands blistering as I pulled them from the earth in flat afternoon heat. You drank it straight from the saucepan. Sunburnt throat moving under the metal. We were sitting in the kitchen together, two stools pushed close. Your eyes were watery. You did not touch me. On the counter, three sardines spilled their guts.

"Are you dying?" I asked you.

"No," you said. "In many ways, I have never been better."

lia

CONFIRMATION COMES IN the shape of his bloodstained shoe washed up high on the shore. Mother finds it, but we don't salt it or burn it the way we would with other dangerous waste. "This is your **father**!" she screams at me when I suggest it. So instead we pull on latex gloves and we all touch the blood patch on the shoe, and then we bury it in the forest. We fling the gloves into the shoe's open grave and Mother fills it in with a shovel. I cry on to Grace's shoulder until the flesh of it shows through the material of her dress, but she only stares into the canopy above us with dry eyes.

"Can you feel something, for once?" I whisper to her later in the dark, sharing her bed without asking permission.

"I hope you die in the night," she whispers back.

Often Grace is repelled by me. I don't have the luxury of being repelled by her, even when her breath is sour and a gentle scum of dirt clings to her ankles. I take whatever contact I can get. Sometimes I harvest the hair from her brush and hide it under my pillow, when things get very bad.

Grace has a deep fascination with a pair of black patent sandals that one of the women left behind years ago. She straps the sandals on from time to time even though the soles flap loose, the leather scales and flakes. One morning she puts them on and lies facedown in the sweating dew, right in the middle of the garden. When Sky and I find her, roll her over with our hands, she is motionless for thirty seconds or more. Her eyes are fixed. Her first movement is to rend at her hair, and we join in like it's a game, but it turns out it's a cue that I didn't even know I was waiting for. Then we are all just useless there on the lawn, already painfully overgrown, waiting for Mother to find us.

Because we are new to mourning, Mother

is panicked. There are no therapies for this unknown crisis. But she is a resourceful woman, ardently repairing the broken her entire life. More than that, she was a woman at our father's side, absorbing and refining his theories. Her hands are bloodless when she lays them upon us. Soon a solution is found.

For one week, Sky and I share Grace's bed. For one week, Mother puts the small blue insomnia tablets on our tongues three to four times a day. Short and foggy breaks in the sleep to be slapped awake, to drink from the glasses of water that crowd the bedside table and to eat crackers Mother spreads with peanut butter, to crawl to the bathroom, because by the third day our legs can no longer be relied upon to hold us. The heavy curtains stay closed to keep the light out, to keep the temperature down.

"What are you feeling?" Mother asks us during those swims up to consciousness. "Good, bad? Oh, I know that I wish I could sleep through all of this. You are the lucky ones."

She monitors our breathing, our pulses. Sky throws up and Mother is there immediately to tenderly scoop the vomit from her mouth with her forefinger and thumb. When she puts her into the bathtub to clean her up we are dimly aware of the shower running like a distant storm.

All through the long sleep my dreams are boxes filled with boxes filled with small trapdoors. I keep thinking I am awake, and then my arms fall off or the sky pulses a livid green, I am outside with my fingers in the sand and the sea is vertical, spilling its seams.

After, it takes a few days for my body to feel normal again. My knees still crumple when I stand. I have bitten my tongue, and it swells and moves in my mouth like a grub against dry earth.

grace, lia, sky

WHEN WE EMERGE from the lost week, we are surrounded by pieces of paper with Mother's writing on like reminders. They are pinned to the walls, slipped into drawers, folded into our clothes. The pieces of paper say, **No more love!** Her pain gives her the gravity of an oracle. We are very troubled by them. We ask her about them and she tells us a revised version.

"Love only your sisters!" All right, we decide, that is easy enough for us to do. "And your mother," she adds. "You have to love me too. It's my right." OK, we tell her. It is no problem.

grace

SOMETIMES WE PRAY in the ballroom, sometimes in Mother's bedroom. It depends on whether we need bombast, Mother on the stage with her arms raised towards the ceiling, sound bouncing from the parquet. In her bedroom it is a quieter worship, graver. We hold hands very tightly, so we can blur where the **I** ends and the **sister** begins. "Devotions for the women of our blood," we say.

It feels good to wish my sisters only well. I can feel them focusing on our love like a crucial piece of information that needs memorizing. "Sometimes," Mother tells us, when she is trying to be loving, "I can no longer tell you girls apart." Some days we like this, some days we don't.

. . .

14

The first time we gather to pray in Mother's room after your death, I broach the idea of drawing the irons again. When I say it nobody nods, nobody agrees with me. Our eyes go to where they hang on her wall. Five hooks, five lengths of iron. Five names above the hooks, but only four names on the irons.

"Once a year, Grace," Mother tells me. "Just because you don't like the result."

Lia looks sideways at me. She was the one who drew the blank iron, which meant that there was no specific love allocated to her this year. "Bad luck," we told her. She was stoic. All of us put our arms around her and told her that of course we would still love her, of course, but we knew it wouldn't be the same, that she would have to scramble more for the affection, that it wouldn't come as easily. We wouldn't be able to touch her so freely. You picked me, as usual, tying me to you for another year. You rigged it. The whole thing was a sham.

"My person is dead," I point out.

"Grief is love," Mother says. I expect her to be angry, but she looks panicked instead. "You could call it the purest kind."

So much for loving only my sisters.

15

It occurs to me that I would like you to come back to life so I could kill you myself.

"We always love some people more," Mother explained when we first drew them. "This way, we can keep it fair. Everyone gets their turn." It seemed simple, with those irons new in our hands and our names painted fresh upon them. Lia got me, that time.

We would all still love each other, but what it meant was: if there was a burning fire, if two sisters were stuck in the inferno and they were screaming a name, the only right thing would be to pick the one the iron dictated to save. It is important to ignore any contrary instinct of your traitor heart. We were quite used to that.

lia

ONE MONTH AFTER we lose our father, King, I am standing at the edge of the swimming pool, in the lavender light that comes up where the border hits the sky. Our pool is the sea made safe, salt water filtered through unseen pipes and sluices, blue and white tiles surrounding it and a marble counter where drinks were once served. Thick rivets of salt are laid down on the tiles immediately bordering the water, guarding against toxins brought in on the wind. King explained to us that the salt drew out badness like damp, his hands quick and busy as he scattered it, tanned a deep, dry brown.

I am wearing a white cotton dress, fishing weights sewn into the hem, the sleeves, the neckline, where their coldness presses against my collarbone. I have not worn it since King died. On the pastel-striped recliner behind me, my belongings: towel and water, sunglasses, an enamel cup of coffee. Taking a deep breath, I release myself into the water.

Grace and I are the only ones who play the drowning game. Sky is more than old enough now, but Mother kicked up a fuss when King suggested that she start—the baby, the favourite—and Mother herself has always been exempt. She has suffered enough already. There is little we can do to save her body now, beyond the palliative. When we were younger she made a point of watching us from one of the recliners, a tall glass of water in her hand, her favourite blue linen dress hitched up to mid-thigh.

Grace and I could go together when we first started. King held us both under the water with ease. He only invented the drowning dress later, when we became bigger, our limbs harder to manipulate. My sister was small for her age, and when I was twelve and she fourteen we overlapped, a year of being exactly the same size, before I overtook her. I remember this as the golden year, the year of my double. We wore identical swimming costumes that

Mother had sewn by hand, red with a bow at the left shoulder. Our lungs started to develop the capacity of grown women, so that we could hold a note for a long, long time. We could blow our emergency whistles for what felt like whole minutes.

My feelings are limping, wretched things. Underwater, staring at the stained tiles, I scream as loudly as I can. The water kills the sound. Opening my eyes, I turn on to my back and watch the sun through the water, a rippling orb of light. It is at times like these that I can imagine holding myself down until the water floods my lungs, that I realize it wouldn't even be so hard. The real trick is how and why we continue surviving at all.

My chest starts to hurt, but I stay under until the static creeps at my vision, and then I claw to the surface. I stagger out of the water, fall on the recliner and wait as the feeling subsides. A deep gratitude floods my heart.

Part of what made the old world so terrible, so prone to destruction, was a total lack of preparation for the personal energies often called **feelings**. Mother told us about these kinds of energies. Especially dangerous for women, our bodies already so vulnerable in ways that the bodies of men are not. It was a wonder that there were still safe places, islands like ours where women can be healthful and whole.

"We've cracked it," King told us in the first days of the drowning game. Inventing a new therapy always put him in an expansive, joyful mood. He whirled Mother around in his arms, her shoulder blades tight against his hands, feet off the floor. Day of happiness! We ate a whole packet of chocolate wafers to celebrate, only slightly stale, dipped in goat's milk.

The air did become lighter; small seabirds came to our home, hovered around the garden, the pool, and sang to each other. Yet beyond the forest, beyond the horizon, the toxin-filled world was still there. It was biding its time.

grace, lia, sky

IN THE HEADY DAYS without our father, we let our bodies sprawl. We no longer breathe into jars so King can test our toxin levels, our lips clamped around the glass. Mother relies instead on circumstantial evidence. On our temperatures, our pulse, the slick and pimpled paleness of the insides of our cheeks. She prescribes double rations of tinned meat, kelp boiled down in the pan. She browns the Spam in oil to fool us into thinking she has killed Lotta without our permission, taking a crowbar to her tensile skull down by the beach. "Cruel!" we shout at the top of our voices once we've established the goat is not dead after all.

Mother often talks about the possibility that one day we will kill her in her sleep, if we don't cause her death indirectly from a heart attack, because daughters are hard-wired for betrayal. How we feel about this statement varies.

"How much do you love Mother today?" we ask each other, one by one, lying in the dying grass of the garden or on the beach, burying each other's feet in the sand. The answers come with no hesitation.

"Two per cent."

"Forty per cent."

"One hundred and twelve per cent."

grace

MOTHER SENSES OUR disquiet, decides to resume order. She lists the chores on a large blackboard in the kitchen, propped up against the yellowing tiles of the wall behind the counter. We erase the words with our hands as we complete them, in no hurry.

Making up our beds with hospital corners, flat and true. Opening the windows and doors on calm days to let the unstirred air in. Cleaning the surfaces in the kitchen with diluted bleach and vinegar, carrying buckets upstairs, sluicing each en suite in turn. Strengthening the salt barriers at the end of the shore, around the pool. Feeding and milking Lotta. Wiping the windows of the sea spray that webs them. The repetition kills me. Every time I rinse my vinegar-pruned hands I ask myself,

Is this all there is now? Just let me lie in the long grass at the end of the garden. Let me sleep through the rest of my days.

Before chores we perform our morning exercises. We stand in a row on the wet lawn, our backs to the heavy ballroom doors. If the weather is not good we retreat to the ballroom itself, the sound of our exercises echoing on the parquet. I am not allowed to do the dangerous ones any more.

Instead I watch as Lia and Sky are left to fall and crumple into the grass. They know what's coming, but still they scream if they make contact with the ground. Mother stuffs the muslin into their mouths to fell the sound. The key thing is that they are falling. There is no hesitance in their limbs. The nature of the game means that they do not always fall: they are caught more often than not. Mother wraps her arms around them and staggers, moves backwards.

Lia and I have been mistaken for twins in the past, but when I watch my younger sisters now I notice how their eyes are identical, their eyelashes sparse and pointed around pale blue irises.

"You should be relieved," you said as I

cried in front of you for what would be the final time. I was not relieved then and I am not relieved now. The dead weights of them, falling backwards in front of me. All you were ever doing in the last days was making me unknown to myself. Revealing thing after useless thing.

We move on to the next exercise, Mother rolling hard, varnished balls for us to swerve away from or catch in our hands, red and blue. She aims to crack them into the bone of our ankles. We have to remain alert to escape the quick explosions of pain. Not me, not any more. I only join in with the stretching and even this makes my back hurt. I have to furl myself up slowly and put my hand in the small of it, and Mother notices.

"Do you need to rest?" she asks me without interrupting her own bending, her body a shivery, wasted thing. "You shouldn't overdo it."

"I'm fine," I tell her, but I don't go back to stretching. Mother raises her arms with no comment. I see all the veins standing out along them. She is showing off to me, I think. She is demonstrating that even her old body is painless, superior to mine.

When the exercises are over I put my arms

around her to make up for my thoughts. Sky joins our embrace, her cheek against my upper arm. Lia stays where she is, doing extra stretches, interlinking her hands and pushing the air away from her. I feel bad that she can't join in our circle. Mother switches her eyes over to where Lia moves and I can tell she is feeling bad too, but there's nothing I can do.

My bed used to be placed next to the wall, Lia's mirroring it in her own room. But as we grew older I started to feel uncomfortable being hemmed in from any angle. Now the bed has to be in the centre of the room. Lia moved hers too, copying me. Sometimes I press my ear against the wall to listen to her breathing, though I would never admit it.

Tonight, I hear her crying. She cries the way she does when it is just us sisters, the three of us alone, and I am surprised. So it isn't for show, that sound pressed from deep in her throat. My own eyes stay dry and I don't go to her, even though I could.

lia

STRONG FEELINGS WEAKEN you, open up your body like a wound. It takes vigilance and regular therapies to hold them at bay. Over the years we have learned how to dampen them down, how to practise and release emotion under strict conditions only, how to own our pain. I can cough it into muslin, trap it as bubbles under the water, let it from my very blood.

Some of the early therapies fell out of favour, and the fainting sack was one of these. King disdained it as archaic. Also, we turned off the sauna years ago to preserve electricity and without the sauna it didn't work. That was a shame in some ways. I enjoyed the dizziness, the rush of my uncooperative body dissolving into nothing.

We use electricity so carefully these days because of the blackouts. They happen most often in the height of summer; the rooms become cavernous after sundown, dotted here and there with the light of candles. I thought this might be a clue to what was happening beyond our borders, but Mother said that she and King orchestrated it themselves, that it was just another part of their plan to keep us safe.

Our fainting sacks were made of a heavy weave, not muslin but not quite burlap. They had once held flour or rice, Mother unstitching the fabric then re-stitching it into the right shape, carefully embroidering our names on to the front. On therapy days she would lead us out in single file, through the kitchen door to the old sauna hut at the edge of the forest, its panels splintering amid flourishing weeds. We held out our arms, naked except for our underwear, and stood motionless while Mother guided our limbs through holes in the rough fabric. She sewed us into the sacks right up to the top of the neck. Then we were carried into the sauna, locked in and given a small glass bottle of water each that quickly became warm as blood.

Soon the sacks were soaked through with our sweat, our own personal salt water. We grew dizzy and lay down on the benches lining the walls. I finished my water first, because I had "poor self-control," as diagnosed repeatedly and sadly by Mother and King. As I sweated out the bad feelings, a lightness came over me. I would allow myself to lick the skin of my forearm once, twice; a reluctance to let my pain go.

Gradually, one by one, we each lost consciousness. When Mother came to rouse us, splashing water on our faces, we shuffled unsteadily on to the lawn together. We were glistening, our hair wet. We lay on our fronts on the grass, the damp fabric chafing at us. She took a pair of scissors to each sack, cutting right down to the bottom along the seams. When we were well enough to stand, we shed the stiff, cooling fabrics to our feet like a skin.

grace, lia, sky

SOME OF THE beds in the abandoned rooms are arranged strangely, left by women long gone. Women who preferred to sleep by windows, or who wanted to keep their eyes trained on the door at all times. Women who were plagued by visions, whose hearts pained them in the night.

We are lucky, because we have been exposed to minimal damage. We remember what those women looked like when they came to us. But we also remember the effect the therapies had on them. How their bodies strengthened until they were finally ready to undergo the water cure.

We only bother to make up our own beds now, stripping the sheets and blankets from the others for our use, so the mattresses lie naked and fleshy on their frames.

"Do you miss the women?" Mother asked us once. To her we answered, "No." Only later, alone, admitting to ourselves, **Yes, maybe a little.**

grace

IN THE LENGTHENING time after your death, I think about the other people who have left us. All women, sickened and damaged when they arrived, cured when they departed. There is a different quality to your absence. A heaviness to it, a shock at its centre. The house is emptier than it has ever been before.

As far back as I can remember, these damaged women drifted through our lives. They arrived with possessions wrapped in sacking, plastic bags, large leather cases that cracked at the seams. Mother would greet their boats at the jetty, looping rope around the moorings.

In reception the women wrote their names and reasons for coming in the Welcome Book while Mother found them a bed. They rarely stayed longer than a month. They ran their hands over the front desk, fake marble but still cold to the touch, in what I now see was a kind of disbelief. At the time we waited in the dark, high up on the stairs, balling dust from the carpet between our fingertips. We weren't supposed to go near the women when they were newly arrived from the mainland with their toxic breath and skin and hair. We fought the urge to make a commotion, to make them turn around and look up at us with their red-rimmed eyes.

You, too, stayed far away from the women, at least at the start. Acclimatization was necessary. They sat waiting with their hands pressed between their knees and their eyes on the floor. They had been through so much, though we had no comprehension of what.

The work started at once. There was no use in letting the body falter longer than necessary. In the dining room Mother laid out two rows of glasses on one of the polished circular tables. Buckets on the floor. We were not supposed to watch.

The women drank the salt water first, their faces pained. They threw up repeatedly into the buckets. Their bodies convulsed. They lay on the floor but Mother helped them up, insistent. They rinsed their mouths, spat. Then they drank from the second row, glass after glass of our good and pure water, the water that came from our taps like a miracle, the water that the sprinklers cast out in the early dusk like a veil across the garden. The water we ourselves drank by the pint first thing every morning, Mother watching our throats as we swallowed. The women took it into themselves. It was a start. The water flamed their cells and blood. Soon the glasses were all empty.

Once Lia and I saw a damaged woman run down the shore towards the jetty. We watched her from the window, waiting for Mother to follow, the way we knew she would if we tried to escape. The woman had bare feet and her hair was the bloom of a dandelion, whipping in the sea wind as she moved her head from side to side. I never knew her name, but something within me now thinks it might have been Anna or Lanna, a soft sound, a name ending with a kind of call. She found her own boat and we saw her get in, we saw her fumble with the motor-string, we saw her leave. She sailed in a curved line across the bay, soon out of our sight. We waved, pressed our hot hands against the glass. We did not know much, yet somewhere we knew that we were watching the beginning of the end.

lia

GRACE'S STOMACH GROWS, filling with blood or air. I notice it first when she is in her swimsuit, sunbathing next to me. I stare at her through my sunglasses until she realizes, bunches a towel across her body despite the heat. At first I think it is a disease, that she is dying. The stomach swelling comes with a deep exhaustion, Grace falling asleep where she sits, circles imprinted under her eyes.

It affects me. For once I am able to keep my distance, she doesn't have to push me away when I get too close to her. I hurt myself more often in an attempt to make some unspoken bargain, line up strands of my hair on the white linen of my pillowcase as votive offerings, but her body still changes. I send out small pleas when I am drowning myself, when I am sponging the blood from my legs. **Save my sister! Take me instead!**

"Thinking yourself uniquely terrible is its own form of narcissism," King had always reminded me, when I went to him crying because nobody loved me any more.

I will probably do anything, I tentatively promise the sea, the sky, the dirt.

"Fetch Grace a glass of water," Mother tells me. "You make the dinner tonight."

I go out to harvest herbs from the garden, spot a small black snake sunning itself on a patch of scrubbed earth. Normally I would scream, but this time I find a branch that has fallen, hit the snake until it's burst open like something cooked too long. I throw salt on its pulp and wash my hands in bleach solution. The skin of my index fingers peels, both hands. **Good enough yet?** I ask nobody.

After we eat, my sister retches in the corner of the lounge. She runs out of the room and down the corridor towards the bathroom, her bare feet an urgent slap on the parquet. When she comes back, her face is like the moon. She lies down right there on the floor, choosing the rug with the tassels in front of the empty fireplace.

I worry that my biceps aren't strong enough to dig her grave and if not me, who will? I worry that I will catch it. I pinch my nose and gargle salt water until my eyes run.

grace, lia, sky

MOTHER IS STRICTER than King at first, but she does relax over time. In the evenings she trickles a small amount of whisky into her glass and drinks it out on the terrace, looking over the rail to the pool below, the treetops just out of reach. We join her out there, and sometimes she tells us about how we arrived, the story of how we came to be.

She tells us about Lia, a stone in her stomach dragging her body down. She tells us about Grace, bundled in white. She tells us about Sky, as yet unimagined but already there, somewhere, in the two that came first. In the dust of the stars above them, or planted in their hearts like a seed. King drove the boat, watched out for dangers, while Mother held Grace in her arms, the burden of two small lives. Another boat was tethered behind, low in the water and almost overladen with belongings, with hope. Neither Mother nor King looked back across the waves, the world shrinking to a flat line, a smear of light and smoke. This was a promised place, is how she tells it. A place that was hers from the start.

grace

DIFFERENT PARTS OF the body submerged mean different things. Different temperatures, too. Ice-bucket therapy for hands and feet, where energies concentrate. Crucial to take the heat of feeling out of ourselves. Naturally cold, I am rarely prescribed it. **Icy little fish,** your pet name for me. Former pet name.

Lia has a day where she can't stop crying, and she doesn't try to hide it. On the contrary she sits in my bed even though I don't want her there.

"You'll poison the air," I tell her, irritated.

"Leave me alone," she says, bunching the duvet around her feet. It's a very hot day. I can see every speck of dust where it twists against the floral wallpaper, the light. Her cheeks are too red. She is fractious, always so difficult.

Mother fills up the ice bucket, half ice, half water. The four of us are in her bathroom. Mother is in her bad-day uniform: King's old grey T-shirt and leggings with holes at the knee. We are all in our nightgowns; we didn't bother getting dressed today. Lia is still crying. She puts her hands in the bucket voluntarily. She wants to feel better. For a second I am moved. "Good girl," Mother murmurs. She keeps her hands on Lia's wrists as my sister closes her eyes and grimaces. Sky drums her hands on the floor, a mosaic of blue and white, does not take her eyes off Lia's face. Her movements become quicker. "Stop that, Sky," Mother says. Lia's own hands move in the bucket, the clumsy sound as she stirs the ice. I watch the colour recede from her face. Air greenhouse-still, browning foliage laid on the windowsill. We are forever bringing flowers inside and forgetting about them, a failure to care about anything other than ourselves.

Later, I go to the pool with Sky. Her body is not a burden to her, and I am jealous. She lies by the pool with her arms flat to her sides, face obscured by the sunglasses you brought back from the mainland. Her skin does not prickle like mine, too tight. There is nothing sloshing and mysterious inside her. When I sit down she puts her arm around me at once and I do not mind it. Her touch is easy and thoughtless. Sometimes when Lia grasps for me it is like we are both being tortured.

I'm surprised Mother has not appeared yet. Normally if my sisters and I are by the pool she can't bring herself to leave us alone. She does not go in but instead lies by the water, inert under a glistening layer of the tanning oil we aren't allowed to use. If we're swimming she will get as close as she can to the water without touching it. We can't even escape her there.

Sky takes off her sunglasses and stands up. "Watch," she says. "I've been practising." She walks to the end of the diving board and meets my eyes, waits until I nod, and then throws herself up into the air. She turns a somersault and hits the water cleanly. She wants nothing from me but my admiration. I give it, because if this world belongs to anybody it is her.

"That was a good one," I say. She flops back

next to me, examines the new spider veins of my legs with a sad noise. The twelve years between us are heavy with the things that a body can do or have done to it. Heartburn leaves a tidemark at the back of my throat every time I eat. My back freezes and tells me **enough**. I can tell she is fascinated and afraid. It has been a while since she has grown at all.

She shifts on to her stomach to let the light catch her back. Fists up her hands in the way that I remember from when she was a baby, when she was carried everywhere in her trailing white sacks with the ceremony of a gift. And I am happy for a minute, here, with my sister, her blameless body reminding me that not everything is in vain.

lia

ONCE EVERY THREE months or so, King went out into the world to fetch supplies. It was a dangerous journey that required careful preparation of the body, so he developed an ingenious system of short sharp inhales and long exhales to propel the mainland air as far away as possible. His face became red as he practised in the ballroom and we joined in solemnly, panting in solidarity; the slatted morning sun falling over us, the curtains of the stage drawn back so that we faced its dark mouth. One of us daughters always fainted. Sometimes it was two or all of us. When that happened, King would become agitated. "You see?" he would tell us as we surrounded the fallen sister, as we flicked water against skin. "You see how quickly you'd die out there?"

On the day itself he would pack the boat with food and water for the journey, with the cross-stitched talismans we created, red and blue thread embroidered on remnants of old bed sheets. The patterns were abstract and mysterious, and he sold them to the husbands and brothers of sick women on the land, who saw hope or magic in the dreamy repetitions of our hands.

King prepared himself by dressing in a white linen suit that was slightly too small, soiled despite Mother's attempts to wash it, the underarms stained yellow. "Function over style," King told us a long time ago. Nothing else that fitted him was reflective enough. He wrapped white cotton around his hands and feet and took wide lengths of muslin to clutch against his mouth.

We all gathered at the shore to cast him off, watching as he walked slowly down the jetty. Crying was allowed on those days because it was our father, and he was taking responsibility for our lives. We looked back behind us at our home, a home kept safe by this and other such actions, and our gratitude almost hurt. King raised his hand to us once he was safely in the boat. When he started sailing we began the breathing exercises again with extra vigour, heads and hearts light. We lifted up our arms. Were we imagining it, that haze on the distant ocean, that barrier he had to cross? Perhaps.

Soon he would be out of sight. He went in a straight line for a while and then turned right until he had left our bay. We knew his lungs were robust enough to filter out some of the toxins, even if his large body became weakened by the air's assault. When Mother started crying we all patted her with our hands.

There was no formal dinner on the leaving days. Instead we ate crackers, the last of the tins, Mother opening more than usual because new things were coming to us: household objects, and food that would keep, sacks of rice and flour and sometimes hard pieces of enamel jewellery that King would place in Mother's palm and she would fold her fingers over. Gallons of bleach in blue canteens. Our own specific requests: soap, bandages, pencils, matches, foil. I always asked for chocolate and was always refused, but I tried every time. Magazines for Mother, handed over in three layers of paper bags and handled lightly by us sisters, who were forbidden to read them.

The journey took three days. One day to reach the mainland, one day spent there, and back on the third. On King's return date, we waited all day. In the morning we helped Mother prepare a Welcome Back meal, our fingers raw and quick against stained plastic chopping boards as we cut onion until it looked like rice, the transparent scatter of it browning in the pan. We concentrated on the chopping with our entire hearts, and when we had finished one onion we would look up before starting the next, gazing out of the large windows that took up most of the kitchen's far wall, searching for the speck of his body.

At dusk we would finally spot the boat and arrange ourselves on the shore to greet him. He returned to us reduced, and it was important for us to hide that it was difficult to see this, so we made sure to keep smiles fixed upon our faces no matter how red his eyes, the hair already covering his chin without his usual routine of a dawn shave, a predinner shave. He always smelled foul. Luckily he never wanted us to touch him upon his return, not even Mother. We unloaded the boat as he dragged his body upstairs to soak in the tub, to let the scum of the outside world fall away. By the time he came back down for dinner he was a little livelier, although with deep circles under his eyes, like someone had taken a chisel to his face. And by the next day he would be back to normal, his regular size, though he still kept his distance for a few days, in case he'd brought something back, and so we were reminded of how easily damaged we were. As if we could forget it.

Once I was caught opening one of the magazines. Mother had left them in their bags on the old reception desk, distracted momentarily by some domestic emergency. Sky saw me reading it and screamed with true fear for me, bringing the others running. Though I didn't make it past the second page I was still required to wear latex gloves for the rest of that week in case I contaminated anyone, and I was banned from dinner for the rest of the week too. My sisters brought me discs of sweatily buttered bread and dry fish that they had hidden in their laps. Grace accompanied her offerings with strict words about how stupid I was; Sky brought hers with sincere guilt about raising the alarm. I forgave her easily because the scream was proof of concern, of love, the same way she would have screamed had a viper been raising its head, fangs bared towards my outstretched hand.

grace, lia, sky

A PIECE OF PAPER pinned to the corkboard in reception is headed simply **Symptoms.**

> **Withering of the skin.**
> **Wasting and hunching of the body.**
> **Unexplained bleeding from anywhere, but particularly eyes, ears, fingernails.**
> **Hair loss.**
> **Exhaustion.**
> **Trouble breathing. Tightness of the throat, the chest.**
> **Agitation.**
> **Hallucinations.**
> **Total collapse.**

There is no hiding the damage the outside world can do, if a woman hasn't been taking the right precautions to guard her body. Mother could always tell from the first moment a new woman arrived how ill she was, whether she was beyond saving, and she would shake her head at the futile hostility of the world, the impossibility of it all. It wasn't their fault that their bodies were unequipped.

"We have young girls," she would tell the newcomer from behind a muffler, the muslin bunched over her lips. Perhaps the woman was just agitated. A nosebleed might have afflicted her on the crossing, blurred drops of blood still lingering at her sleeve from where she had dragged it across her face. "Please wait down on the beach, just to be sure."

Sometimes all they needed was a few hours of the new air to improve. From the window as they rested on the shore, heads pillowed on their luggage, we could almost see their strength replenishing, the way it did with King when he returned to our land. We watched their shoulders straighten, the shaking of their bodies subside.

grace

THERE IS A violence to our eulogizing. We are making something of you that you never consented to. We are turning you into something else: a man finally overcome by the world. I know you would not want to be remembered that way. Thinking about you is akin to dragging your bloated ghost to shore. And why would we want to keep bringing that back?

Lia creates a shrine. Her hands do not shake as she arranges photographs and cowrie shells, even as her eyes leak. I let her have the comfort and do not comment, just look at the tattered photo that is you and Mother on your wedding day, a flower crown, the white suit when it was newly purchased.

Shrines are banned, Mother writes in

yellow chalk one morning, the chalkboard propped near the breakfast table so we can't ignore it. **Stay present. Stay with me.**

These days I am thinking a lot about your approach to life-guarding, your declarations that you would fell anyone if necessary, in the name of love. And even during the bleaker nights I can hear how the baby inside me sings, or seems to. Popping and amniotic, like the calls of dolphins.

lia

ON A HUSHED EVENING following a hushed day, Mother takes us into the ballroom and leads Grace on to the small stage at its far end. "Your sister is to have a baby," she tells us. We applaud and march our feet on the floor to drum up noise, but we make too much of it and Grace winces.

"Where is it from?" Sky asks.

"Grace asked the sea for one," Mother tells us, her hand hovering at the end of Grace's braid. "She has been lucky."

I stare at Grace until she meets my gaze. How dare she.

Later I climb over the rail of the terrace and pull myself up to sit on the roof itself, the edges of the slate tiles digging into my thighs, and I watch the dark sea. I ask and ask, but there is no answering call inside my own body. The waves remain the same, the thinning evening air does not stir. It is possible I want it too much, the way I want everything.

When we were younger, Grace and I played a game called Dying. It involved folding your body over and wadding your eyes up tight. It involved shaking. I was always the one who died—of course I was—so I lay in front of my sister as she threw salt on me.

"We told you not to go out in the world!" Grace would shout in an imitation of Mother. "What did you wear?"

Just my body. Just the gown.

"You're shrinking now," said Grace, strictly. "Your lungs have burned up. Your eyes are drying out. Soon you will disappear."

Please.

When I walk past Grace's room later on, I see her lying unmoving on her stomach, the soles of her feet filthy against white linen. I think for a second that she is dead, but when I call she kicks her feet listlessly, assures me that she is very much alive.

grace, lia, sky

TIME WITHOUT OUR father becomes stretching, soft. Sugar melted in the pan and drawn into something new before hardening, contracting. There are many days which bleed into each other. The sun in the sky seems closer to us all the time.

Incidences of joy like playing hide-and-seek together, on a rare raining day. Water rinsing the walls of the house, pouring to the drains. From the tall glass doors of the ballroom we watch it pooling on the ground, and filling empty burnt-earth pots that once held small, fragrant trees. Then we move to conceal our bodies. We discover each other wrapped in a velvet curtain, in the old industrial oven, unused for decades, petrified grease caking its ceiling, or behind furniture or doors, waiting patiently for a long time.

Sometimes we become mildly sick, headaches or stomach cramps, and if one sister is sick it's like we are all sick, so we rally our efforts into healing. The afflicted sister lies on the bed and we brush her hair, administer the small white pills that King brought back encased in cardboard and bubbles of foil. When the sister is better, we cheer. **Look what we did,** we tell each other. **Look how we fixed you.**

grace

I GO DOWN to the forest whenever I can shake my sisters off. The only place I can find a degree of calm is among the sightless trees, their shadow.

Slipping from the house and across the lawn, I move stealthily through the ornamental beds, past rocks marking out the borders of vegetable patches we no longer maintain. The green beans stopped growing years ago, but the tomatoes, nearer the house, have taken on a life of their own. Their fruit falls and attracts stinging insects. A jam of dirt, overblown globes and seeds.

Down at the end of the garden, I pull up my skirt and climb over the low wall. This is where the forest begins. There is no birdsong, only the dry-skin noise of the leaves. On the other side, I run my hands along the stones of the wall until I find the right one and pull it out. Matches, wrapped in cloth to keep them from damp. A small lighter that belonged to you, yellow plastic. I try it out experimentally on a pile of dead twigs, the liquid inside low, but it still works. For a second I remember how your hands looked moving the flint, the flame rising up, and something passes over me. I do not cry. **Fuck you,** I mouth to the air instead. It makes no reply. Where is your ghost when I need it?

There is barbed wire in the forest, deeper than I dare to go. Should anyone arrive on the island, it serves the same purpose as the buoys out in the bay, marking out a clear message. **Do not enter.** Viewed from another angle, **Do not leave.** I imagine the smoke drifting over it, a defiant signal. But I am too far away, and I stamp it out within minutes. I wonder what it would be like to set the whole forest on fire, to see everything curl up and blacken. But this small blaze is as much as I would dare to do. There is no real danger. The woods will always have the coolness of shadow, dark and wet underneath the boughs.

. . .

60

Beside the pool in the afternoon, Lia will not stop talking at me about you, the word **remember** repeated on the wind like an incantation. She idolized you.

The desperation in her voice is unbearable. Eventually I slap her and she almost falls, then comes back up towards me with her hands ready to fight. I lean back.

"I'm not going to hit you!" she tells me, horrified at the idea, despite her automatic fists. They are just a reflex. "Not in your condition!"

I go inside to sit in the cool alone, but I slam the door behind me too hard and the ancient chandelier falls from the ceiling in a plume of plaster dust. Glass ripples out over the floor. I scream and scream until everyone else is standing around me, staring, too dumbfounded by my reaction even to run for muslin to stop up my mouth.

"This house is going to kill us," I tell Mother. She has no qualms about hitting me in the face then, condition or no condition.

lia

TWO DARK PURPLE fingertips on my left hand, from being submerged in ice. The dead big toenail of my left foot also.

The comma from a paperclip I held in the flame of a candle, pressed against the baby skin of my inner upper arm.

The starburst at the back of my neck where Mother once sewed my skin into the fainting sack. Two stitches. She did it on purpose, and yet somehow the blood when I ripped them out was my fault. I want to die every time I think about it.

Bald patch near the nape of my neck, size and smoothness of a fingernail. That wound belongs to King, who pulled the hair out with his own hands.

Large red stain on my right thumb. This is

the thumb I press to the hob when I am cooking. It helps.

Water mark on my flank. Mother poured the hot kettle on me. I screamed bloody murder. I punched her square in the jaw and she just grinned, a pink-tinged grin, because I had caught her lip against the teeth but caused no mortal harm.

grace, lia, sky

WHEN THE DAMAGED women saw King for the first time they often recoiled. **Man.** But our mother explained that here was a man who had renounced the world. Here was a man who recognized the dangers. Here was a man who put his women and children first.

Away from the toxins, a man's body could swell and develop unchecked. That was why King was so tall. We thought the hair on the top of his head might grow back too, but it turned out that was a damage that could not be reversed.

"What are men beyond the border like?" we asked him.

Eventually he gave us an answer. He spoke of perverse appetites. He spoke of bodies grown strong despite the toxic air, men like trees grown against the wind, knotted, warped. Some thrived on the poison; it was like their bodies had learned not just to overcome, but to need it. He spoke of danger. Men like that tracked around the toxins carelessly. You would feel the effect in their breath, the touch of their hands. Men like that would break your arm without thinking. "Like this," he had said, demonstrating on us, clasping both fists around each of our forearms in turn and making as if to snap. We felt the bone threaten to give, stayed calm. "And worse."

grace

THE SEASON TURNS about five months after your death and there comes a higher tide than usual, water pressing up against the coastline. An annual occasion. The sea rushes forward to cover the jetty, engulfing the shore and swelling right up to the pebbles on the shingle line. Mother consulted the almanac a week ago so we knew it was coming. We gather in the lounge to watch the swollen moon from the window. The light feels purifying.

I think about the things that have washed up to us on previous high tides. Squat catfish the size of my arm, rotten as a blister. Jellyfish full of poison. Other things that we were not allowed to see, things that meant the beach needed to be cordoned off, our curtains closed. Tides dredge and bring forth. The world comes nearer to us.

"Careful, girls," Mother instructs us. She is letting us watch for now because it is beautiful. Because of the light's quality. When I glance to my side I see Lia's eyes wet with tears. Sky's eyes are closed, and I close my own eyes too, picture my heart flipping in my chest. Underneath that I picture the baby, lying still. Even through closed glass the air smells of pine and salt. It almost burns.

The next day comes house arrest as Mother patrols the shore. She puts on King's white linen trousers, the fabric falling over her feet, a muslin veil hanging down from a wide-brimmed hat to cover her face. It looks elegant. She will check the tideline, the shallows, even the edge of the forest, though the water never rises that far. She locks the front door behind us. We lag in reception, watching her pass through the door, watching the handle turn, the click of the key. The world outside seems to glow with a new and clean light.

We go to the lounge. Mother has let down the curtains but not the blackout blinds that cut out sunlight completely. Lia goes to the window, but Sky calls out "No!" with such fear that she doesn't have the heart to push it. Instead she comes back and kneels on all fours so that our little sister can ride her like an animal, even though Sky is really too big for that now. They move mournfully around the room, Lia dipping her head so her dark hair reaches the floor, gathers there like a rope being let down. In the end they lie on the carpet and stick their limbs into the air, moving them around.

"Woodlouse," Lia says as she watches the movement of her arms and legs, slow, controlled. It was our old game. "We are stuck and cannot get up."

Soon Mother comes back to tell us we are safe again, but we decide to keep all the windows and doors closed anyway, just in case. Mother nods at our caution. "You are doing so well," she tells us, taking off the hat. The muslin trails to the ground. "I am so proud of you."

lia

TRAUMA IS A toxin that hooks into our hair and organs and blood and becomes part of us, the way heavy metals do, our bodies nothing more than a layering of flesh around everything ingested and experienced. These things sit inside us like the misshapen pearls we sometimes prise from oysters. Fear calcifies in our veins and the chambers of our hearts. Pain is a currency like the talismans we sewed for the sick women, a give and take, a way to strengthen and prepare the body. "You think you know pain," Mother used to say. "You don't know anything, you have no idea." And then the love of the family, a balm that keeps our airways soft and wet, a thing to keep us drawing breath.

There has always been the worry that I

would catch something of Grace's trauma, because she was exposed young, at the age when any trace of toxin would cause immeasurable harm, whether or not she remembered it. Mother and King were traumatized too in their own ways, but they spoke of adulthood like a mantle, something that repelled.

Scream therapy then, in the early days, was supposed to tap our feelings out of us, allow us to expel the excess through the mouth. Up on the terrace on a windy day, we stood in the air. King still had some of his hair back then, nestling at the ears. I remember him being a giant, remember the wind bending me and Grace. Mother wore earplugs and held her arms around us, supporting us in the hot gusts. King held a stick that he called a **conducting baton.** He stood a few feet away from us, no earplugs, all the better to check we were screaming with the correct cadence, with sufficient enthusiasm.

"Scream from the chest," he had told us. "Low down. None of that throat-screaming. Not through the nose."

We did. The air came out of our mouths, heavy, full.

"Louder!" shouted King. The wind was

taking the sound away. I would never be able to scream loud enough. I launched my voice with all my force and felt unendurably happy. I had been waiting my whole short life to feel that way.

"Now move to a throat scream," he told us, lifting the baton higher. We adjusted how the air was being expelled. The shrieking was high-pitched now, a noise of terror rather than of fierce joy. The baton moved from side to side, Grace screaming more powerfully, and then me. My voice cracked slightly. Our mouths were dry.

"One final push," King encouraged us. "One last go. Give it all you've got."

A pause, a breath. We gathered ourselves and then we let loose, we opened our mouths as wide as they would go and the blood flooded my face, there was no more air. My cheeks were wet with unexpected tears. It was such a relief, to do that. It was such a relief.

grace, lia, sky

WITHOUT OUR FATHER, it is very hard not to think about things going wrong. Years ago we saw something forbidden—something that washed up in a storm, one of the times when Mother had locked us in the house and drawn the curtains tight. But there are so many rooms here, so many windows. When she went outside we simply found another room at the top of the house, and through the glass we saw the lump that Mother and King were digging a hole for. What could only be a ghost, fat and blue. It had been a woman, was now the nightmarish memory of a woman. It was undoubtedly toxic and yet we could not look away.

Mother was surrounded by the damaged

women and they were crying hysterically, all of them. But King did not cry. He was grim and resolute. As we watched he covered the ghost with a sheet and drove the shovel into the sand like it was an enemy he was killing.

grace

I AM WALKING towards your grave when I notice the browning of the leaves. It's too early for the summer death of the greenery. I move through the forest carefully, noting other changes. When I come to the border, I can see it has rusted badly, some parts almost broken.

I have a theory that pregnancy ramps up your ability to intuit a threat. Extra-sensory. Mother has a theory that pregnancy makes you histrionic. I am milky, hormonal, prone to sticking cold teaspoons in my mouth so I can taste the metal.

I have tried to discuss the border with Mother, but either she doesn't want to know or she doesn't want to talk about it with me.

It causes me a lot of stress to think about pushing the wet lump of my baby out into a compromised world.

lia

THERE ARE SOME things I thought had died with our father, but I am wrong. Mother tells us over breakfast that we will be heading down to the shore for a love therapy, and I have to put down my spoon. Suddenly I am not hungry. The slick orbs of tinned fruit, anaemic, swim in their juice. A prune like a dark yolk next to them. Grace continues to spoon mandarin segments into her mouth, unperturbed. The therapies are never as bad for her. Her hands never tremble when she puts them in the sack, when she moves to draw an iron out.

As we approach the beach I see two small cardboard boxes with air holes in the lid and a large bucket next to them, several gallons' capacity, already full of water. Also a smaller bucket, a box of matches, a pile of twigs and leaves, and two pairs of thick gardening gloves. Sky grasps for Grace's hand and I twist my own behind my back.

"My girls," Mother says. Her face is speckled from the season, from the heat, her eyes like two pale chips of glass against the skin, her lips cracked. She always loves this, seeing us being brave. She gestures for me and Sky to come forward.

"Lia, you first," she tells me. The one with the least love always starts it. I pull on the thick gloves. She ducks to the floor and picks up both boxes. "Choose."

I take one from her and hold it in my hands. Something inside runs around, the box's centre of gravity moving. I place it on the sand next to me, and take the other. Something is in this one too, but it is slower. Dank woodland smells from both of them. I put it down.

"I choose the first one," I tell her. Get it over with. She nods.

"It's a mouse," she says. "I found it this morning in the traps." She looks from me to Sky. "Sky, take the box."

Sky picks up the first box. The movements become quicker, a scuffling at the edge of the box. Her hands are shaking.

"You can let Sky drown the mouse," Mother tells me. "Or you can do it for her."

Sky looks at me imploringly, but she doesn't need to. I am already reaching for the box even though the idea of the small velvet body makes me want to cry, the thought of it moving in my hands. My sisters watch me mutely as I lift the lid.

"Don't let it get out," Mother tells me, but in one motion I cup it under the stomach, lift it out and drop it into the bucket of water. It flails valiantly but it is already exhausted. Soon it sinks and lies motionless, suspended. I feel the tears gather at the back of my throat. Sky mouths **Thank you** to me, water in her own eyes.

The next box holds a toad, leathery and stunned. I know Sky would be terrified of holding it but I have no such problems, stroking its squat body with one gloved finger, hoping that might be it. Mice are pests, spreaders of disease, enemies of our survival. Toads are not. But Mother gestures to what I now realize is kindling, next to the box of matches on the sand.

"Mother, no," says Grace. "That's too cruel."

"Life is cruel," Mother tells her. "If you girls can't make difficult decisions for each other now, you'll never be able to."

I look down at the toad, its ugly skin. Its movements are slow, as if the warmth of my hands is comforting.

"Mother," I say too. My mouth is dry.

"If you won't do it, your sister has to," Mother says.

"Please, Mother, no!" Sky says, on the verge of tears again. "Please don't make either of us do it."

"I'll touch it with my bare hands," I tell her. "I'll drown it."

"No," she says. "I don't want you getting sick. And it can swim. I wasn't born yesterday." She looks to my sisters. "Get the fire lit, then."

When the bonfire is ready, I crouch next to its small flames. Mother is looking at me, seeing if I will go through with it. I could let the toad go, hurl it down the beach. It might die then too, its body smashed and useless. My breathing is ragged.

"If you can't do it, give it to Sky," Mother says one last time. But I will not make my sister do this, and she knows it. I drop the toad into the fire and move back.

Almost instantly, Mother throws a bucket of water over the flames. The toad hops out, barely blackened.

"You passed," Mother tells me. "Well done."

Sky looks up at me, stricken with gratefulness. Our feelings pass between us like an electric charge. I accept them, absorb them, and then the weeping comes over me in a wave and I pull off the dirty gloves, put my hands to my face.

grace, lia, sky

THERE ARE STILL days when Mother doesn't get out of bed, though they are further apart now. On those days we know she is thinking of King, and we know that she is suffering from a thing called heartbreak that we have no comprehension of and probably never will. She tells us this not-knowing is a gift, like the life she managed to breathe into us, the life she has always protected so fiercely.

"Can you not be grateful for that? Can you not thank me for that?" she asks us from the bed, her blankets a smudge in the darkness as we stand in the doorway.

We say, "Yes, Mother. Thank you, Mother."

grace

"DRAW PICTURES OF what the men have done to you," Mother told the damaged women. Lia, Sky and I were allowed to sit in on this kind of session, occasionally. "So you don't have to let the words out." The mystery of it. I wanted to look at every page, but the women shielded their pads with their bodies as if the information were deadly.

They hunched over their paper, pencils and pens moving in wide arcs. It was a busy season. Seven or eight of the women were staying with us at that time, looking at us daughters with watery eyes across the breakfast table, or standing out at the edge of the forest with you and Mother, holding hands loosely, staring into the dark.

"You can keep it abstract, if you want,"

Mother told them, benevolent. The varnish on her nails was chipped. She looked tired. She went from woman to woman as they drew, tapping their shoulder before she looked.

"May I?" she asked them, and then studied each page in turn.

Putting the things down on the paper was better than letting the words into the air, which would be tantamount to bringing the contamination with them. We didn't see the pictures. One woman wept, tore a hole at the centre of the page. Another drew something in great detail and spent the rest of the afternoon rubbing it out carefully, centimetre by centimetre.

Later we were allowed to join them on the shore as the drawings were all burned, the women throwing matches and salt on the bonfire. You always kept your distance, surveying from the back. You must have wanted to look. The drawings were not things you had done, but the actions belonged to you the way the pain of the women belonged to us. Your body made you a traitor, despite everything. We stayed there until the tide came up and reached the ashes, turned them into sludge.

lia

AFTER YEARS OF them, I am used to sudden awakenings, to Mother's hand clamped against my mouth. Always a drill for some unspecified event, the worst ever yet to come, always her dank vegetable breath and the white space of her eyes, blinking too fast. I go with her every time, even when my sisters refuse, feign too-deep sleep, charm her into letting them stay put. Being asked is enough for me, let alone the possibility that this time it could be real. Fear roiling in my stomach, and something else too, something close to hope. Every year the seasons become warmer and it is the earth telling me that change is coming, it is the air whispering, **It will not always be so,** and in the meantime this intimacy as I follow Mother down the stairs when nobody else will, the cool torchlight, for to be good is to be loved, I do believe this, and I have been good, I am always being good.

There is a storm the night that it finally happens. Mother wakes us up, will not take no for an answer, and leads us into her bathroom. It is cramped, too hot, blankets and pillows on the floor for us to use as bedding, but the only window is small and has a wooden blind that shuts out all the light. King made that blind himself so he could develop photographs in the pitch-dark, dripping paper over the bath. Mother floats tea lights in the sink. We try to make a bed for Grace in the tub but she is too large now to fit in, bulbous like an insect with her skinny legs, so in the end Sky is the one who lies down in the porcelain with a folded towel beneath her head. Grace stretches out on the floor, my hands hovering above Grace's stomach. My need thrums uncomfortably loud. "Don't," Grace says. She does not say it gently.

Water from the tap, our mouths kissing the metal directly. Water scattered with our fingers at each other, cooling. Mother stands and tries to see what she can from the window.

When the wind catches the blind extra hard she makes the same shushing noises that King had developed for his trips, her lips pursed, as if she can out-blow it. To the noise of the rain, the noise of the protections of our mother, we fall into curled-body sleep.

In the morning the storm is over and Mother is gone. The three of us wake each other, move slowly through the door into her bedroom, where she stands by the window, looking down at something on the beach. She is shaking, and I start to shake too. I cannot help it.

"Stay there," she tells us without looking around. "Don't move."

We ignore her, walk to the window. "No," she says again, but it's too late.

There are three people lying on the shore, high up on the sand past the breakers. As we watch, one of them sits up and retches ungracefully into the sand. They remain sitting up.

"They're men," Mother says, putting her arms out to push us back, though they are far below us, though we are safe for now. "Men have come to us."

part two

men

Thank you for opening your home to me. It is very difficult to feel that there is no hope, that all there will ever be is pain and no cure. I should have known that sisterhood would be the answer. I look forward to getting to know the others.

lia

EMERGENCY HAS ALWAYS been with us; if not present emergency then always the idea that it is coming. The ringing in the air after a loud sound has passed. The count before the thunder hits. And here, finally, is the emergency we have been waiting for our whole lives.

We gather lengths of muslin and our knives and we move down to the shore while the men are still weak. By the time we arrive, they are sitting up. Two grown men and one boy, all of them tracked with salt and sand. The small one is crying hard. We stand in a semicircle a safe distance away from them, fabric bunched in our hands, ready.

One of the men gets to his feet. His body is elongated, dark hair across his chin and head, cropped close. The other man is older, shorter, his hair fair or grey or both, pale eyes that he shares with the first man. A blue rucksack, soaking wet, lies on the ground between them.

"Please don't be afraid," says the man who is standing up. His words come out differently from ours. He extends a hand though we are too far away to take it, though we wouldn't take it anyway.

"Stop," says Mother. He withdraws the gesture immediately.

"We had an accident," he says, swaying slightly. "Our boat went down." He gestures to the sea, but there is no wreckage.

"You shouldn't be here at all," Mother tells him. "This is private property."

"We're looking for sanctuary," he says. "We know of your husband, King. Can we speak to him?"

Mother's face looks uncertain.

"Girls, go further up the beach," she tells us. "Move back."

We do as we are told, until she raises her hand.

"Men," we whisper to each other, our heads almost touching. "Men men men." We are appalled. My legs shake. I turn to see whether I can make out teeth, claws, weapon, but there's nothing to suggest their danger.

After some time speaking, she gestures for us to return.

The strangers are standing now and Mother displays the knife casually, as if it's just another part of her, a part she knows extremely well.

"Why shouldn't we drown you?" she demands.

"Would you drown a child?" the dark-haired one asks in return. He pushes the boy forward. My sisters and I clutch at each other. The boy is sweet. His eyes are pink, rabbit-like.

"I would do anything for my girls," Mother says, stoic.

The men look at the water. It is calm, but there are currents that would take you under in a second.

"We can be of use," the older one says. "We can protect you."

"We don't need protecting," Mother says.

"You might do soon," the dark-haired man says. "This isn't a threat from us, understand. But a lot of things are happening out there. People worse than us could be coming for you."

Mother seems to consider this.

"Perhaps this is fortuitous," he continues. "We are fathers, we are husbands, like he was." So she has told them. A quick stab of grief passes through me. He looks at us. "We know something of how to keep people safe."

The boy sits down abruptly on the sand, as if his legs have given way. The older one places a hand on his head.

In the time since King, we have not rigged a single trap. In the time since King, we have let the patrols slip. We have not killed the animals that could be harbouring toxins. We have become softer already, worn by the burden of vigilance. But Mother is not hasty. She knows all about the lies and exhortations of men.

"We need time," she tells them. "Until then, you stay here. Where we can see you."

The dark-haired one stares at her. "Where will we shelter?"

Mother shrugs. "The storm is over."

"Could we please have some water?" asks the older man.

Mother gestures at the sea. "Knock yourself out."

. . .

"Are we going to let them die, then?" Grace asks with rare interest when we are back in the house, sitting at the table for breakfast as if nothing has happened. Mother locks the dining-room doors, and the kitchen door, normally open at all times. We'll see them if they walk towards the moorings, but neither boat is big enough to hold three men. The remaining motorboat, gleaming white and red, will carry two at most. The rowing boat takes on water and is for short journeys only.

"Let me think, Grace," Mother says.

"Maybe they are friends of King," Grace continues, ignoring her. "Maybe they have come to pay their respects."

Mother puts her hand to her head; the stress of it all has given her a migraine. The sick voltage of the pain drifts from her left eye over the entire side of her body, and though she would usually want to be alone she insists now that we all stay together until it leaves her. We sit in her room for hours with the curtains closed, checking periodically on the men from the window, holding our breath throughout the plush mid-afternoon dark. Grace puts a wet cloth on Mother's forehead. When she has passed out for good, the three of us watch the men from her bathroom window, together. The dark-haired one is knee-deep in the water, shirtless, his back to us. It must be very hot now. The small one is lying on the sand like something that has been spat out. The older one has his knees to his chest, and like the child he is not moving.

We stand guard in shifts through the night. When it is my turn I walk from room to room on the ground floor, exhilarated. My mouth is dry. In the kitchen I am sitting on the tiles, black diamonds against terra-cotta, when the knocking starts, the shadow of a man at the door leading into the garden.

It is the dark-haired one and the child. They watch me, blurred, through the glass. The boy is crying again, his face alien and liquid, and the man mouths a word at me, which I realize is **Please.** I am not used to being offered this word. It is a spell, a weakness. I am moved; I let them in.

It is just a step over the threshold, the matter of a few inches, outside versus in. The man doesn't hesitate, pushing the child in one fluid motion as if afraid I will change my mind, which I could, which I should, and then both of them straighten up and look at me, making direct, unprotected eye contact with me for the first time, and their eyes are shadowed holes in their heads, containing something that I cannot comprehend.

"We just want water," the dark-haired man says, quietly and urgently. "Maybe some food, if you have it. Then we'll go."

I turn my back to them and fill one glass, then another, at the sink. The proximity of their forbidden bodies has a gravitational pull. They drain the glasses and I fill them again. I find a milk bottle and fill that too. The dried fruit I was going to eat—figs from the garden, splitting hearts laid out on trays in the attic to shrivel and crystallize—I hand out without touching their skin. And then they do go, they are out of the door without looking back, and I step out after them, I am watching, I am still standing guard.

Mother is renewed in the morning, post-migraine. Everything smells better; she asks for bread and butter, for apples and tea. A vision came to her in the night. It was King, and he told her to **show deep kindness for now and for always**. They were swimming in the pool, meeting underwater in the middle of it. Mother woke up before they could touch. She cries a little as she tells us about it, a dab of water under her eye.

"You mean you had a dream," Grace says.

"You can't swim," adds Sky.

"You are both cruel," says Mother. She splits the skin from an apple slice with her thumbnail, peels it off in one vulturous motion.

We are not supposed to see what she does to the men, but we watch from Grace's room, which turns out to have a good view. Sky and I stay ducked down at the window, our hair all in our faces and mouths. Grace keeps up a running commentary, her voice distant.

"She is making them take off all their clothes," she says.

We strain our eyes to look. There the men are, pulling off their T-shirts and jeans. Mother gestures. She is holding King's pistol up to them. They take their underwear off too. Their skin is striped with different colours, like ours, but that is the only thing we seem to share. I am grimly fascinated. Grace makes a small sound of disgust.

"She is checking their clothes and rucksack

for weapons," she continues. Sure enough, the men have backed away and Mother is lifting their limp garments, shaking them with great vigour and letting them drop.

"She is pointing the gun at them again," Grace says. I wish she would be quiet. We can all see Mother after all, her arm raised, clearly right up close to them now. They try to shield themselves with their hands but she must have instructed them to stop that, to press their arms close to their sides, their bodies exposed.

We meet them properly for the first time at the dinner table, when they enter the room dressed in clothes that belonged to our father, clothes which are too big for them, even though the grown men are at least a head taller than any of us. We are sitting already when they come in, but we rise to our feet, ceremonial. I touch the square of muslin folded up in my pocket, just in case. The men line up on the opposite end of the table to us, sunburnt and weary. Mother stands at the head.

"I'm Llew," the dark-haired one says. He puts a hand on the shoulder of the boy, next to him. "This is Gwil. Say hello."

Gwil moves his feet, looks at each of our faces quickly, then to the grimy ceiling. "Hello," he says.

"I'm James," says the older one. "Gwil's uncle. Llew's brother."

I am surprised and happy at the idea that blood ties them together; it feels like some kind of familiarity. We say our own names, in order of age.

"Sit," instructs Mother, and we do as we are told.

The men eat quickly, too quickly. I worry they will choke. Llew shucks oysters and slides them on to his plate and on to Gwil's. There's something about the smoothness of his movements, his eyes luminous and quick. His arms have a fur on them that disgusts and enchants me at the same time. Grace kicks me under the table sideways when she sees me looking.

Llew teaches us how to pronounce his name, but none of us can do it. I resolve to practise it secretly so I can impress him. Drops of condensation roll down the wineglass that holds my water.

James asks me how old I am, and I shrug. When he turns his attention to Grace and asks how far along she is, Mother takes the opportunity to preach about the superiority of daughters. We shuffle in our chairs.

"Do you have daughters?" she asks the men.

No, not yet, they tell her. **Maybe one day**. She is disappointed. Grace murderously dismembers the tail end of the fish.

We eat in silence for a while. Mother seems to be debating whether or not to say something. In the end, she puts down her fork.

"Nobody comes here any more," she tells them. Her voice is lowered, but we can all still hear her. "It's not like it was before." She pauses. "So, I don't know. You need to make your own way from here."

I think of the damaged women in the boats with their thinning hair, their strange voices and gifts wrapped in brown paper. The translucent skin at their temples, at the backs of their hands.

"They'll come," Llew tells her as he takes more food. His voice is kind. "They'll find us. We just need to stay here for a few days until they do."

Mother doesn't say anything more, just lifts the fork to her mouth. I want to cry at the ease with which they know they will be found.

After dinner, we go about the rituals stealthily. Mother distracts the men with playing cards, fanning them out on the dining table and encouraging them to play. We leave the room through the tall glass doors and watch the shadows of them moving against the wall, arms reaching, the unfamiliar hum of their voices falling away. We pick our way down to the shore with salt cupped between our palms, and we lay it down with the usual care.

It is just before I go to sleep, the sky still light, when I see a strange bird pass overhead. It is not one I've ever seen before, and I look up in awe at the stiff wings, its shadowed shape dark against the sky. It's far away, yet I can hear the drone of its song very faintly through the open sliver of my bathroom window. Grace is in her room and I call for her, I run to her door and knock on it until she follows me. She stands on the toilet seat to get a better angle, but she only catches the last seconds before we can no longer see it. I wonder where it nests, whether it flies endlessly or bobs on the waves, pulling together a raft made of the faltering world's debris. Grace finds my hand with hers, and we link fingers tightly for a second before she pulls away, as if remembering that we no longer do that.

We have never been permitted to cry because it makes our energies suffocating. Crying lays you low and vulnerable, racks your body. If water is the cure for what ails us, the water that comes from our own faces and hearts is the wrong sort. It has absorbed our pain and is dangerous to let loose. **Pathological despair** was King's way of describing an emergency that needed cloth, confinement, our heads held underwater. What constituted an emergency was me and my sisters crying in unison, unable to stop.

I love to cry, though. With King gone, I have forgotten to feel guilty about doing it. There is no one left to notice what I do now. Alone in my room, the windows flung open and the sun lazy against my eyes. Or underwater in the pool, where all water is the same water. Sometimes I imagine the death of my sisters, the image of them standing against the rails on the terrace and paper-crumpling down to the ground, one by one, and then the tears come even when I remind myself that they are still alive. It's important, the knowledge that things could always be worse. Imagining them gone makes the edges of my love sharper. In those moments I almost understand what they mean to me.

The night the men come, I cry quite a lot without knowing why. My sleep is shallow. Their distant bodies are thumbprints of heat, somewhere lost in the house.

My husband left the village. My brothers left. Everyone else's husbands, brothers, sons and fathers and uncles and nephews left too. They went in droves. They apologized for leaving. There was danger in them. They hoped that we would understand.

IN THE MORNING I pace the corridors outside our three bedrooms as if to set a boundary. We used to say that any yellow patches on the carpet are made of fire; if you stepped on them you would burn to death. I step carefully all the way to the window that looks out on the forest, lean my forearms on the sill. The air where it comes in is a sweet and clean thing, but some of the trees are going brown, dying. **Vigilance,** I whisper to myself. I press my ear to each of my sisters' doors so I can check their breathing and am just about satisfied.

From the top of the staircase I can hear distant piano music. I expect to find Mother clearing her mind, but when I enter the ballroom it is Llew, facing away from me. The bulk of his shoulders, hair shorn from his neck. It's a shock, like seeing a snake dart into the scrub of the forest. His hands fumble the notes as he turns, and I realize he is scared of me too, or at least who I could be in this moment. Mother with the pistol. Vengeful women coming to catch him off-guard. He and the piano are perfectly placed in a hot rectangle of sunlight.

"It's you," he says. "The one who gave us the water."

I nod.

"Did I wake you?" he asks. I shake my head. "Good." He indicates the piano. "Can you play?"

"No," I say.

"Why not?" he asks.

I shrug.

"It's out of tune anyway," he says. "That'll be the sea air." He cocks his head to one side. "I don't bite, you know. Come over here."

Mother discussed with us the importance of examining every action of our bodies. Step always with caution. The body is the purest sort of alarm. If something feels wrong, it probably is. My body does not pulse with fear, though my hands shake a little. I am curious, that's all. The man smiles at me as I start to walk.

Llew makes room for me on the stool. Even through his clothes he is warmer than a woman would be. Like my father, he is made of meat. It's not so terrible, to be close to him. I put a finger to the keys, pick one at random. He takes my lead and chooses a key near mine, makes a harmony, and then picks another.

"Anyone can learn piano," he tells me. "Babies can learn it. Old people. It's not too late for you."

I have never learned it because I am clumsy and uninterested, because the sound of the notes puts my teeth on edge, creates a hard ball of sorrow in my chest. I don't need that, I could tell him, I am sad enough already without it. But I let him teach me a very simple tune that I manage to remember. I play it once, then twice, faster each time. He congratulates me, but it's only fifteen notes, it's no great achievement. He sucks air in between his teeth, which are a lot whiter than mine. "See?" he says.

When the door opens again, it is Mother; I can tell without even seeing. I stand up right away, but Llew does not move.

"Good morning!" Llew greets her. Mother ignores him.

"It's breakfast time," she says instead, fixing her eyes on me. "Everyone else is awake now."

Llew puts the lid of the piano down without

comment, pushes the stool back. There is a fluidity to his movements, despite his size, that tells me he has never had to justify his existence, has never had to fold himself into a hidden thing, and I wonder what that must be like, to know that your body is irreproachable. I try to follow him out of the room, but Mother grabs my wrist as I walk past her. She says nothing but gives me a look, her eyes narrowed almost shut.

For a second, I hate her. I want to lock my fingers around her throat. Then I remember as I always do that I am supposed to love her, so I look back into her eyes and think of an orb of pink light, my obedient heart.

Over breakfast, Mother lays out the new rules. She has been up all night recalibrating, fighting with the world around us. She implies that we should feel guilty about this. We test our mother's spirit, hurt her without even realizing. Daughters are always thankless, we know by now. You could cut yourself on the sharpness of our disregard. We're vain, senseless, arrogant. This morning I'll admit I did pull the skin around my eyes to test the elasticity, I did put on the whitest dress—vinegar-bleached, eyelets at the hem.

"No daughter to be alone with a man," she reads from her notebook. "No men to go near the daughters' rooms. No men to touch the daughters, unless sanctioned by me."

What would be enough to sanction touch? I wonder, I feel my sisters wonder. If we were drowning, maybe. If there was a wad of bread, a fishbone, lodged in our tender throats. I imagine formulas and workings-out scrawled in the margins, calculating how much our bodies can take before unspeakable damage would be done to us. I worry at a scab on the back of my right hand, a wound I don't remember. In the new light streaming through the windows, a light there's no hiding from, I can see the lines at James's eyes more clearly, the fading plumpness of Gwil's face. Llew's arms are folded as he leans back against his chair. When I look at his body properly I feel sick, but also exultant. I realize that if I have to stand up in front of him I will fall and give myself away.

Mother draws out King's pistol from underneath the table, and places it on the tablecloth.

"If you touch the girls, I'll have to kill you," Mother says. She is relishing it, unapologetic.

"Right," says James. "We understand." He puts one hand on Gwil's shoulder and looks at Llew.

"Loud and clear," says Llew, smiling at Mother, and then at the rest of us.

Mother claps her hands. "Well, now that's sorted, let's get on with the day. Girls, I need you. Come with me."

The men remain inside as we follow her out to the jetty. The air is dry, all moisture burned off by the ferocious sun reflecting off the flat sea. Sweat breaks out immediately on my forehead, the back of my neck. Reaching the far end, Mother holds the pistol up high. We sway with the rhythm of the water under our feet.

"You remember this," she tells us. "Well, now is the time for you to learn how to use it." She reaches into her pocket. "This is a bullet. Look." She opens the gun, puts the bullet in, closes it again.

She turns around, pointing out to sea, and aims at nothing. There is a great bang that moves her backwards a little, a spiral of smoke rising, and Sky clutches at Grace. Nothing else happens.

"If you fire that at somebody, they will die instantly," Mother explains calmly. "It's the most effective way to kill a person. Point it at the head, or the chest." She rubs her shoulder.

Mother has us all try out the pistol, even Sky, who cries when it knocks her on to the wooden boards of the jetty, but only for a few seconds. I try to keep my arm exactly steady and don't move my eyes from the middle distance even when the jolt runs through my entire body, much stronger than I expect. We fall quiet, listening out for a sound after the bang, but nothing comes.

When we turn to go back the men are watching us from the shore as if attracted by the noise, and there is something that might be relief on their faces at the sight of us, far away but unharmed.

Later I go out on the boat alone. No sharks nose at the wooden hull. They aren't interested in me, in my bitter heart and bones. I hope that if they killed my father, the flesh of him made them sick. Muddy seaweed moves on the water's surface like wet hair. When I'm out a safe distance from the shore I drag my skin against an exposed nail sticking from a plank, leaving a faint red mark that evaporates even as I watch it. King warned me once about lockjaw, rust infecting the blood. This isn't the way to do what I need.

Instead, I put my palm against a metal joint in the wood, steel that has soaked up the heat. Better, but nowhere near enough. I pull up a netful of writhing silver fish and let them die in the bottom of the boat, watching them as their breathing grows more desperate. Eventually it stops. **I know the feeling,** I tell them.

Our world is made up of humid air over rough sea, riptides theoretical and deadly, birds that hew the blue sky with their ominous bodies. The dark frieze of the forest wraps around the edges of our vision, a reassuring bank of oak and coastal pine—names King taught me, as he cut strips of crumbling red bark to hold in my hand. And at the centre our home, glaring at me now from the middle distance, white and huge as a cake. From here it still looks like a house that will save you, that could at least get you partway there.

Many women have banked on that promise

and laid themselves down on white linen, shut the blinds against the sun and the air, rested themselves. The years have been long without them. Soothing memories of soft female voices, cool gusts of air from the open windows of the lounge, feet stuttering over floorboards, chairs pulled up into the middle of the ballroom to watch a speech, a therapy. There have never been any men before. Men didn't need what we offered.

When I return to the shore, the boy child is inspecting the shallows, careful not to get his feet wet. He is poking a stick into the sand, methodically, as if searching for something. His wrists are spindly, his mouth pinched. I keep my distance, turning over pebbles with my feet until something catches my interest: a smooth green jewel or piece of glass, clouded with age. It fits perfectly inside my palm and I slip it into my pocket, because even the unlovable deserve something, because I take my gifts where I can find them.

Higher up on the shore I find a dead bird, black feathers flecked with green. I notice it because of the flies, their sound and movement around it. It's just on the edge of the tideline, no way of telling if the sea brought it in or it died in our own sky. I keep my distance for a while before deciding to blow the whistle around my neck. Mother and my sisters come quickly, spilling out of the door and over the sand towards me in white and blue cotton. I raise my hands to them.

"A dead bird," I shout. "Dead."

"Get away from it!" Mother calls. I don't need telling twice, backing further away. We stand around it in a wide circle. "Fetch the salt, Lia."

Llew is in the kitchen when I run in, leaning on a stainless-steel counter, eating cornflakes by the handful. He sticks his hand right in, lifts his palm to his mouth and tips his head back. I make a mental note to throw the packet out.

"What are you doing?" he asks, mouth full, as I dump the net of fish on the table and turn to pull out the Mason jar of salt from underneath the sink. He puts the packet down, plants his eyes very carefully on me.

"Nothing," I tell him. This isn't for him. I manage to walk out of the kitchen, but the second I'm away from his gaze I run again.

The pebbles fall away from my feet. My skin is too hot.

Mother has collected driftwood and stones and debris. She and my sisters arrange it on top of the bird. Gwil watches from a distance, still holding the stick, but we ignore him.

"Salt," Mother orders. I open the lid for her to scoop her hands in and she does, taking a palmful. Sky looks close to tears by now, Grace bored. They take their own handfuls of salt. They scatter it on the bonfire, and I copy them. Mother draws a matchbox from her pocket and sets the kindling alight. We jump back from the flame. A thin line of smoke rises up.

"Oh, girls," Mother says as she watches the crisped seaweed and wood burn. There is a deep mournfulness to her voice. "It's not a good sign."

Her eyes flick to me briefly and I feel the lemon-twist of guilt, the sourness. I know what that look means.

I don't want to play the drowning game with the men lying splayed by the pool as if they were dead, so I go to my room instead and close the door behind me. On the other side of my bed, furthest from the door, I sit on the carpet. Nobody can see me here. I open the bedside drawer and pull out sharp quartz, flint, the razor blades I have stolen from Mother and King's bathroom cabinet. I choose a blade, even though I've been worrying about them running out without King's trips to the mainland. We are noticing shortages in other areas too. I am rationing my soaps, cutting them into cubes with a paring knife. Only the salt will last, harvested from shallow tubs of seawater left to dry under the sun.

I stretch out my legs in front of me, pull my skirt above my knees. The carpet is a nauseous swirl, a pattern that was meant to mimic the forest. The skin drags and reddens, but doesn't break. On the next go it does, springing up a beaded trail of red. One centimetre, two, three.

My body, King said, was the sort that would attract harm, the sort that wouldn't last long elsewhere. But he really meant my feelings, spiralling out from my chest like the fronds of a sea creature. My sisters do not like to see the wounds on me, averting their eyes from the neat squares of gauze, but they understand that it's inevitable. They would just rather not be reminded.

In my bathroom I wash the wounds carefully. Before long, the new blood stops hitting the bathtub and spidering out around the drain. I bandage myself and check my reflection.

I put everything away, then move to the window. Drawing back the curtain a little, I can see the bodies of the men down by the water from another angle. They are white slabs that have fallen from the sky and stayed where they hit, a creeping hair on their chests and limbs. They are far away from me, but still I shrink back as their heads turn. I don't want them to see me watching them. Instead I look out to the sea, gauging the level of the swell, the fractals of the cloud cover. I try to see the ashes we left on the sand, but I am too distant and it is no longer a problem. We have contained the emergency. We have taken the necessary precautions.

Sometimes my housemates, hardier girls, brought men back to their rooms, and I couldn't understand why they did it, whether it was recklessness or inoculation or both, and on those days I wadded a towel at the bottom of my door, poured boiling water into a basin and breathed in the steam.

BY THE NEXT morning, we notice disturbances in the feminine fabric. Subtle warps, new ways of doing things. Like the men standing in the shallows with weapons they have made themselves, knives strapped to sticks that have fallen in the forest, the water lapping at their knees. Grace has not yet come to terms with their presence. She says to me, hopefully, as we watch them from our recliners, "It would be exciting if a shark killed them."

Most of me, a significant most, wants to disagree. I watch how Llew lifts Gwil up by the armpits and swings him around until the child shouts, then sets him down in the shallows and ruffles his hair, batting at him to stay back. It signals something to me, something shocking and good, to see love displayed so openly, so wholly without ulterior motive. I find myself retreating inside to cry briefly in the blue dim of the downstairs bathroom, the mould-smelling hand towel pressed to my face to muffle the noise. Grace can tell when I return with my eyes red, but she does not comment. She looks away from me.

King preferred less obvious weapons than spears. He was a connoisseur of traps, of looped ropes and subterfuge. He always believed there was something offensive in overt violence. It was like asking for trouble, it disturbed things. But all that happens is that the men fill a basket with shining fish and carry it to Mother, who cooks them up. They are delicious. You can't tell they are things that died a traumatic and writhing death.

We do our exercises out on the lawn at midday, when the sun is highest, so Mother can see us sweat. The water pours off me. I feint and roll, move my body into a cat's stretch, hold out my arms to catch Sky under her armpits, lightly, lightly, letting go of her as soon as possible. When I turn back to the house I catch a movement at a dark window and scrutinize it as I bring my leg up behind me, grip my ankle. It's Llew, watching us. There is no mistaking it. He freezes when he sees my eyes on him but doesn't hide. I turn back so Mother won't be alerted, complicit once more.

"Press-ups," Mother says. We drop to the ground, we test the strength of our arms. I can do the most press-ups: I can do ten, twenty, thirty, beyond, my sisters groaning on the ground. I am doing them to tell him something about my body, but when I look back to the window he has gone.

The men have been watching us at other times. At meals they chew and stare, they roll their food around their mouths. Maybe they would eat us given half a chance. Anything is possible with these hungry-looking men. I have been consuming less, nerves twisting in my stomach. They look at our hands when we are sewing in the evening. King is not here to sell the talismans any more, but we keep making them because what else are we going to do? When Mother sees the men looking she stares back at them until they stop. I have not mastered this trick: my own eyes swerve. Llew smiles a lot. There is a kind of softness in him, I can tell.

My body, up until now, has been just a thing that bled. A thing with vast reserves of pain. A strange instrument that I don't always understand. But something kicks in, triggered by the looking. I believe it to be an instinct, not yet sure whether it qualifies to have the word **survival** in front of it.

Now or never, I tell my reflection in the mirror, wearing a dress dug out from Sky's wardrobe, inches above my knees and too tight. I walk slowly across the edge of the pool to be sure that the men will notice my approach, trying something out.

When I reach my recliner I lie on my stomach and look up surreptitiously behind my sunglasses, across the shimmering water, to where Llew rests. As I watch him he pushes his own glasses up and winks at me, before lowering them again. I bury my face in my arms. Mother has set up her recliner at the head of the pool, next to the lifeguard's chair, drawing the line at sitting in the chair itself. She can still survey both sides of the pool, male and female. A scarf elegant around her head, skin streaked with oil.

The grand finale: I sit up, pull the dress over my head and stand for a few seconds in just my swimsuit, pretending to inspect the sky above the fringe of the forest. Heart hammering, waiting for someone to find me out, for something to strike me down, I lose my nerve anyway and cannonball into the water. Sky wails at the sudden break in the silence, Grace moving to comfort her, so when I rise to the surface they are staring baldly at me, arms around each other.

After dinner when we are on the shore as usual, under the darkening air, pouring salt on to the boundary lines, Mother slaps me in front of my sisters. Once with the back of the hand, the rings she wears on every finger catching my ear, and then with the palm for good measure. I raise my fists to hit back and scream as loudly as I can, and at once the hands of my sisters cover my face, my mouth.

"You said no touching!" I shout. "You didn't say anything about eye contact. What else am I not allowed to look at?"

"Don't cause a scene," Mother tells me, as if she hadn't been the one to hit me first. "Come with me."

She walks back towards the house but stops before the shingle, sitting on the damp sand and indicating that we should join her. She takes our hands, even mine, though I have to share with Sky, my hand piled on the top as an afterthought. The lights of the house and the pool shine a way off.

"I know what it's like to be a young woman," she tells us. "I know all about what can destroy you."

We wait for her to tell us more.

"It's natural, what you're feeling," she says, addressing me specifically this time. "It's natural to want to look."

Grace laughs, a short laugh.

"Stop it, Grace," Mother tells her. She squeezes our hands tighter. The men are somewhere inside, I don't know where. In our corridors, breathing our air. Sitting in our furniture, leaving their trace.

"You need a love therapy," she tells us. She lets go of our hands. "I put the Welcome Book in Grace's room. I'll come and knock for you when the hour is up."

As well as the book, Mother has left scarves in Grace's room, thin and silken fabric that falls into large squares when we shake them out. **These are to cover your body,** a note says. **Put these on when you are sunbathing.** My sisters gripe, and it's true, it is undeniably my fault. We lie on the carpet to try them out. They are big enough to cover us from our head to our toes. I pull mine down, claustrophobic. Grace and Sky look like cocoons, only the motion of their breath, a twitch of the arm, suggesting they are alive at all.

After we tire of the scarves, we climb up on the bed and Grace begins to read mournfully from the Welcome Book, reason after reason after reason. Testament of how men hurt women. Testament of the old world. We have heard them all before, many times, but still I close my eyes against them, against the unease and gravity of their prophecy. Sky fidgets, trying to find a comfortable position, but there is no comfortable way to listen. We shudder when we think of how some of the women looked when they came to us. Like they had been bled out, their skin limp. Eyes watering involuntarily, hair thinning.

I became allergic to my husband. He refused to acknowledge how sick he was making me. He told me I was making it up, that it wasn't possible, even when I coughed up blood, when my hair stopped up the plughole. He held me through

the night and by dawn my skin was hard and red where he had touched me. And the rest of it. Leave me alone, I pleaded, can't you do without. He bought me steroid lotion and a gauze mask that did nothing, left me breathing shallowly in the bed every morning.

"Horrible!" Grace says when she has read half a dozen or more. She closes her eyes for a second, exhales very slowly and deeply. It is an unusual reaction from her and I am shaken, more by this than by the words themselves. The Welcome Book is largely too abstract to scare me much, though I am certainly sad for the women and their pain, dimly aware somewhere that this pain is the tradition to which I belong.

Afterwards, we discuss first impressions of the men. **Loud. Oily.** Grace screws up her face in disgust. We are all comparing them to King, our only reference point, our yardstick for safe manhood. They are all shorter than him, I point out. Positive, no? Less air taken up by their bodies. Sweat always dampening the hair at their temples. I don't mention the feel of Llew's arm next to mine, watching the easy spread of his hands playing piano, but I am thinking it, I am thinking it and I am appalled at myself. Sky joins in with the word **friendly,** and Grace bristles.

"Easy to be friendly when you want something," she tells her. "See if you think they're so friendly when they're cutting your throat."

"Grace," we say in protest. "They wouldn't." She throws up her hands, doesn't look at either of us.

When Mother has pardoned us, put her hands on our foreheads to gauge our temperatures and declared us well for now, I shower for a long time. With both hands I soap my hair, letting the suds get into my eyes as penance. I rub a thinning towel across my body and slick my legs with a thick, vanilla-scented cream that Grace gave me months ago, something King had brought back for her from his final voyage. She hadn't wanted it. She knew I would.

Why do you care? I ask myself. Talking to myself is a bad habit I've picked up in the last few months as Grace has become less and less available to me, shutting herself away for long hours in the room next door, changing minute by imperceptible minute.

Now that we have been reminded of what is at stake, Mother allows the men to sit with us in the lounge. My sisters and I stay on the sofa with the sagging heart, Sky draped over Grace, me in the corner with one knee up to my chest, pretending to sew. I stab carelessly at the fabric when anyone looks at me. Really I am just watching Llew with Gwil again. Hands flickering between suits as they play cards, laying them down so quickly they blur. The boy laughs as he wins; the father punches him lightly on the arm. Softly, softly. **Father,** I grieve for a second, knotting my hands too tightly and letting my embroidery fall.

It turns out the love therapy has done nothing for me. Llew puts a glass of water to his mouth; a piece of dark hair falls over his forehead and he pushes it back. Closed eyes, for a second, as he swallows. I close my own. Mother and Grace knit striped things for the baby as Sky pulls a cat's cradle of red cotton between her teeth, between thumb and fore-finger. My sisters, at least, are serene.

When Llew leaves the room, I am bereft. I go to the bathroom to splash water on my face. **Stupid,** I tell myself. **No good.** But he is outside the bathroom itself in the corridor, leaning out of the window, which is open as wide as it will go. Pine mist, silhouetted against the heat of the day burning off.

Despite everything, I did sometimes dare to believe that love would come for me, that it would find me somewhere. It would come from the ocean or the air. It would wash up like the rare plastics inscribed with scraps of lettering, or I would sail to the border and somehow breathe it into me. I have always been a hopeful person. Painfully optimistic, Grace had called me once. It was supposed to be an insult.

Llew doesn't seem surprised to see me. He raises his hand to me, moves sideways to make room. I join him at the windowsill and lean the top half of my body out. He asks about the mountains. They are barely visible through the falling cloud, past the forest, a long way away. I don't know what to talk about, what words could be good enough to interest him. He asks if we could go and visit them, but they are full of animals that kill you and anyway there is no way to do it, so I can't promise anything, I have nothing to give.

"Your mother has been quite cruel to us," Llew tells me. "But you don't mind us, do you?" He stretches out his arms. "I can tell there's not a bad bone in your body."

A wolf almost made it to us, once. King cut its throat and strung its pelt up in the forest as a warning to other wolves. It looked like a giant bird of prey, suspended in motion. Red velvet underneath, then brown. He kept it there until it rotted, and then cut it down.

I can hear my sisters behind me in the room, talking indistinctly, probably bickering. Their voices are a reproach. I should be there with them, safety in numbers, our bodies, our witnessing, some sort of defence. The man moves his body closer to me and I also move closer, why not, why not, I cannot help myself. The warm and rising smell of his skin.

Llew turns to look at me. Half his face is in shadow, his mouth hidden.

"You're very beautiful, you know," he says.

My throat is filled with something. He reaches out to my face and tucks a piece of hair behind my ear, then turns and walks back down the corridor, towards the lounge, without saying anything else.

I fetch a glass of water and drink it alone in the unlit kitchen, watching the clouds move past the moon, then go outside into the garden, turn on to the beach. I don't stop until I feel sand under my feet and then I sit where I fall, splaying my hands into it as if to root myself. The water lies slick and still, a small garnish of foam where it hits the shore. I want Llew to come out after me, but it is impossible.

Once I kept a young rabbit in a shoebox under my bed for three weeks, and I loved it dearly, but Mother found it one morning while cleaning my room. King took the rabbit down into the garden and killed it by planting one foot on top of it, and then he pushed my face into the earth as the sky sweated above us.

Violence from my father, who after all was still a man, was a last resort. Even then my eagerness for love compromised my family. It is terrible to be that person. Mother had to fumigate my room with a heated pan of salt, glowing red. I watched from the keyhole and I can picture her now, stately in white, moving from corner to corner.

We did our best to protect each other—it was necessarily imperfect, but we did try with all our hearts. Who else would try for us? Who else would lie down in the dirt, if not our women, our mothers and daughters and sisters? We were not too proud to get down there.

WHEN I WAKE, my body is useless with grief. Eventually I get up and splash my face with cold water to calm my red eyes, so Mother won't make me use the ice bucket, won't humiliate me in front of the men. After brushing my teeth I stuff my mouth with muslin and hyperventilate, then I put the muslin to soak in my bathtub, three inches of cold water, and let the water drain safely as I lie down on the tiles of the floor, the spare dawn light covering my body from the window.

Be good, be good, be good. A reckoning with my body. **Please, just for one second,** I beg my feelings, lying there, waiting for them to subside.

The men wore hunting clothes, I remember from the Welcome Book. **The men stockpiled weapons in the cellars of their homes, and practised on deer. The men of my home town, the men of my family. Fathers one and all. You could not tell the bad men from the good.**

"So some of them were good!" I say to the air with triumph.

Afterwards, Mother is waiting for me downstairs, alone in the dining room with the remains of breakfast around her, looking out of the window. I feel a little afraid of her, the aftermath of my agitation surely tangible, but all she asks is for me to dye her hair. We change into stained and matching grey T-shirts and go to the collection of dye boxes in her bathroom, hoarded underneath the windowsill.

"Running out," she says, mostly to herself. "Maybe I'll try a coffee rinse next time." She kneels down beside the bathtub, winces at the pressure on her knees. Her feet, soles upturned towards me, are ingrained deeply with dirt. I touch the cheek of the woman on the front of the box, mix up the contents of the bottles. Squeeze the dye into my bare hands, gelatinous and black. I brace myself for another lecture, but Mother just sighs as I massage it against her scalp. She bends her neck uncomplainingly as I rinse with the shower attachment until the water comes clear, her vertebrae exposed. She is not so much precious to me as fragile. She was someone's daughter, once. And perhaps that is what she is trying to remind me. Women together in our vulnerability, her neck presented like a breakable thing. Nothing is mentioned about the men, this time.

I go up to the terrace afterwards, and find Grace already there. I sit next to her and she shifts but doesn't say anything. I put on my sunglasses, draw my bare legs up to my body. When I look down at my nails and palms, they're stained from the dye. I will think of Mother every time I use my hands today, tomorrow, until I scrub them raw.

"How do you feel?" she asks eventually. She is eating dry crackers, half a dozen of them left on a saucer, arranged into the shape of a half-moon. She doesn't offer me one.

"Fine," I say.

"Not sick?" she asks. She puts half a cracker on to her tongue and leaves it there without chewing. "They've breathed all over you."

"You too," I point out.

"Not true," she says. "I've made sure to stay a good distance away when they talk. It's not difficult."

"Well, I feel fine," I say. "Better than ever."

I rest my hand against my forehead, subtly. I am very slightly warmer than usual, a hint of feverishness.

"We can't take chances," she says, once her mouth is empty. "I want them to leave." She touches her stomach. "We don't need them."

"When do you think the others will come for them?" I ask.

She lifts her shoulders. "Maybe there's nobody to come for them at all," she says. "Who would come here if they could help it?" A small bitterness, quickly extinguished.

Would **others** mean even more men, coming in on boats shrouded in shadow? I want to ask her, but I am too excited, too afraid.

Staring at the sky until my vision blurs, I spot another bird. Its trail is faint; it is far away, a sharp gleam in the sky.

"Grace," I whisper.

"What now?" she says, and I point at the strange bird's path above us. She sits up, watches it calmly until it is out of view.

"Well," she says.

"We should tell Mother," I say.

"Later on," she replies. "It's all right." She is being kind now, which hurts even more. She lets down the recliner so she is completely supine and rests the saucer on her thighs, below the bump of her stomach. If she moves suddenly it will fall and break, but I don't take it away from her and put it on the table, I just watch the faint motion of it as she breathes deeply, in and out, until I can no longer bear it.

Every time I think **I am very lonely,** it becomes bleaker and more true. You can think things into being. You can dwell them up from the ground.

The heat builds. Leaving my sister where she lies, I go down through the close, still house and out on to the shoreline, picking my way over shingle and scree. Something to do, anything. The sand meets the trees, marram grass giving way to the cool of birch, of pine, a transitional zone where the heat of the open sky turns into something sheltered, something secret.

I part the high grass with my hands, feel the sting of thorns, of nettles, but ignore it. There could be snakes anywhere, the dislocated yawn of their fangs. I am always alternating between invincibility and the sick fear of dying. Our whole life has centred on survival. It would follow that we are better at it than most. **Arrogance,** King would call this if he was alive. I still keep an eye out for anything that could be his body when I'm in the forest. A viper could have felled him. An unknown enemy could have been hiding in the trees.

Soon the high grass gives way to clearings, patches of dirt. I slow in case of traps left unsprung, and keep an eye out for the marked trees that would tell me where I can and can't go. It isn't long before I see the first warning tree, horizontal gouges cut out halfway up the trunk, and then I wait for a while, sitting on a tree trunk at the edge of a patch of dirt, my nerve ebbing. Flies hurl themselves at my face.

I turn at a noise, and Llew steps into the clearing. Only him. The portion of the forest we are allowed is small, after all. He must have followed me, must have seen me walk trancelike from the house, watched me on the shore. He looks above our heads at the foliage, the green light. Somewhere in the distance something chatters; bird or rodent, I can't tell.

"Where does the forest end?" he asks,

lounging against a tree, and I am not afraid, though aware I should be.

"It goes over the mountains," I tell him. "But I'll show you where we can go to."

We walk for a short while, the notched trees growing more numerous. I feel Llew's hand on my hair, my head, and stop so suddenly that he walks into me.

"A spider," he says. "I brushed it off for you. I stopped it running down your neck. I saved your life." He takes it away slowly, lets his arm drop to his side.

Eventually we come to the first border of barbed wire. Criss-crossing over itself again and again, it is taller than Llew because King was taller than Llew and King was the one who marked it out to his own measurements, his own specifications.

"It's not electric?" Llew asks me. I shake my head and he goes right up to it, touches it gingerly around the barbs and shakes it. It is rusting now. It has been a long time since I have come so close. The other side, through the wire, looks the same as our side.

"If I ask you what this is all about, will

you tell me?" Llew says, and when I shake my head he laughs. "I thought so." He lets go of the wire, kicks it lightly with his foot.

"Show me more," he asks, so I walk with him along the wire border, where it runs parallel to our territory. Soon I point up to where you can see the paint of the house in the distance, shining white, elevated slightly. We are at the back. Our feet disturb pine needles and clods of earth.

"Could we get home that way?" he asks me, and so we change direction. I am glad when the wire is metres behind us, then concealed by trees. Llew walks by my side, lagging just enough to make the hackles rise on the back of my neck. For a second, like coming to, I remember where we are, and that he is an animal I don't know anything about. He seems soft and tender around Gwil, but this does not mean he is a soft and tender thing. He could have a knife in his pocket, concealed, rags to stuff into my mouth. Anything. Ways of killing I have never dreamed of.

"Walk ahead of me," I tell him. He laughs in my face, stops.

"Are you afraid of me?" he asks. He steps closer. I can feel his breath at my hairline.

"No," I say.

"Good," he says. "You don't need to be." He moves as if to take my hands in his, but thinks better of it, arms swinging back down by his sides. He turns around and starts walking again, this time ahead of me by a whole step. He whistles.

I watch him surreptitiously, think about how I could use a felled branch to hit him on the head and kill him flat. I could take a piece of the barbed wire and wrap it around my knuckles, just in case. But then: "Hurry up," he calls, turning his head to me, and I obey despite myself, my feet moving as if he is in charge of them, and I want to cry all of a sudden but I know it is important not to, not in front of him, in this place.

Soon we scale the old stone wall, beyond it the incline that leads up to the back of the house, the beds that were once pristine, now a mess of unkempt roses. At the top there lies a stagnant pond where the mosquitoes foment. On the way I fall on the sloping lawn without him seeing and press my hands against the beautiful earth, the grass and leaves. I want to stay there.

By the pond he holds whole heads of flowers

in his palms. He shakes out the pods of their seeds, stains pollen on his fingertips.

"What are these called?" he asks me again and again. I say the names that I know. Near a wall veined with ivy and honeysuckle, he pauses.

"Romantic," he says. He smiles at me. The smell is too sweet. He pulls a bloom from the stone and hands it to me. "For you."

I let it drop, breathe through my mouth so as not to get the smell of rot, the plants around us choking on their own juice. He hands me another flower, and this time I look at his too-large hands and take it.

"Look," he says, getting to his knees behind the wall. "Come here." He has spotted something on the ground, but I can't make out what. When I crouch down next to him to look at it more closely, he puts his arm around me but I don't pull away. My body is a traitor. I am also a traitor.

He leans in and presses his mouth to mine for a second. When he pulls away I see the thing on the ground is the carcass of a mouse, not long dead. I debate whether to spit his toxicity out on to the ground, but before I can make a decision he kisses me again. Then he laughs, presses his forehead to mine briefly. He stands up.

"Poor thing," he says. He means the mouse. Something has ripped its throat out. He kicks a small pile of dirt and leaves over it. I wipe my lips with the back of my hand. They feel filled with blood, as if I've been hit in the face.

"You can go ahead of me now," Llew says. "Who knows whether you were planning to kill me all along, trailing behind me there?"

When we reach the back of the house I lead him through the peeling ballroom doors, into the room's shadowed interior. Nobody saw us, nobody sees us. We walk through the dim of the corridor together, the falling sun casting washes of light against the walls, and he hovers his long body a safe distance from mine. We no longer touch.

"I'd like to be alone with you," he says, the same way he might say, **I'd like to go for a swim.**

I finally swallow the saliva collected under my tongue, imagine a dark syrup sliding somewhere towards my stomach with a calm that surprises me.

. . .

Before bed, I brush my teeth four times. When I first spit into the sink it is stippled lightly with blood. By the fourth brushing it is mostly blood, and I do not know whether it is his fault or mine, the toothbrush gouging at my mouth. Then I rinse with plain water, not wanting to risk going to the kitchen for salt and seeing anyone, gargling and gargling until every trace of toxin must surely be down the plughole. I cannot rinse the feel of it, though, and I do not want to, despite everything. When the bleeding stops, my gums are pale where I bare them but otherwise unchanged.

I should be thinking about atoning. But all I can think about is how when he kissed me for the second time he put a hand to the back of my head as if conscious of keeping me upright, and he was right, I did think I would fall, the swing of the sky as if I was on the edge of drunk, of something—and how did he know that I felt like that, how did he know to hold me upright, my tilting body, my eyes open wide?

. . .

At early dawn, I think I hear the strange bird return. Its song is an echoing call through the sky. And yet when I look there is nothing, no bird and now no sound either, though I'm sure it was not a dream. I go back to bed and hold my hands pressed very tightly between my knees and count to one hundred, two hundred, three hundred, the bones in my hands moving, a manageable pain that lulls me eventually to sleep.

My initial strategy was to adopt the men's behaviours. I exposed myself to the bad air to try and make myself stronger, still lay on my usual park bench with my top rolled up an inch or two, exposing my ribs. I made my voice louder, so that people winced away from me. I walked with a rollicking, rolling gait.

WE SPIED ON Mother and King in the old days, their weekly dinners alone, followed by pecking at each other like birds on the sand, embracing on the recliners, followed by their move upstairs where they were not to be disturbed. The public acts of their bodies as important as the private, a demonstration to us that they were still very much in love. This ritual comforted me. It happened like clockwork, a scheduled intimacy that Mother explained was how intimacy should be, in a perfect world—never overwhelming, never lacking in joy. Small portions of love, held in the palm like a gift.

In the morning, Mother watches me watching him. Possibly she can read my thoughts, which are considering the possibilities of **alone.** At the end of breakfast, she makes me stay as everyone else files out.

"You're getting sick," she tells me. "You

have to stay in solitary confinement until the afternoon."

"I feel fine," I tell her. She frowns, takes the thermometer from its case on the sideboard and offers it to me. I keep my tongue very still over the glass.

"Like I thought," she says, frantic, holding it up to the light. "You've been spending too much time with them already. When will you learn to look after yourself?"

I follow her up to the bedrooms. We go into hers, not mine.

"Meditate upon the irons," she tells me. "Sit on the floor and look at them."

She leaves the room and locks me in behind her, so there's no way out. I stare at the pieces of metal until my eyes water. Even I have no patience with myself, no actual interest in loving the sack of bones and guts that makes me up.

And yet—there in the garden, with the dirt caking the fabric at his knees and my body balanced on the balls of my feet, ready to fall over at any second, was something new. In a hot rush I realize that love may not be off-limits for me after all. An opportunity.

I know that without being touched I will

die. I have known it for some time. It has always felt like I need more touch than the others anyway, my hands brushing over their shoulders or the tops of their heads as they shy away, because nobody is assigned to me. I am not anybody's loved-most, have not been for some time. I have gone days, weeks, without touch and when that happens I can feel my skin thinning, I have to lay my body against grass and velvet and the corner of the sofa and rub my hands and elbows and thighs against anything until they are raw.

Later, released from confinement, I return to my room and the door snags on a scrap of paper. A note on the carpet. It's a page torn from the Welcome Book in reception, lined in a faint gold. On one side, blue ink in cursive starts, **Thank you for opening your home to me**. On the other side, a black scrawl says, **Meet me at the pool tonight, late. Llew.**

He has been watching to see which room is mine, I realize with disbelief. I read the note five, six, seven times, then start to laugh, quietly, until I have to press my face into the pillow to stop the sound.

. . .

At evening prayers, I stare Mother right in the eye. I look at her the whole way through. She seems gratified, smiles and smiles at me. It is easy to please her, sometimes.

"Invocations for the damaged women, for their strength and peace," we say.

"Love for our sisters and our home.

"Good health for our mother." She presses her palm to her chest, for emphasis.

There are new ones now.

"We pray for protection against the bodies of men.

"We pray for the men's good hearts, for good intentions."

A glass bottle is produced. We line up in a row. Mother places a dropper on our tongues, one at a time, sweetness at the roofs of our mouths. She presses her thumb over the label so we can't read it.

"I can't overstate the importance of keeping your distance from them," she tells us, but she has been wrong before and she could be wrong again, and there is no guilt in my heart tonight, for once.

I see him illuminated from some distance away, swimming backstroke in the glowing water. I moved without sound through the sleeping house, past the bedrooms of my sisters, my treacherous heart beating loud and true. We are too visible out here at the pool, yet still I slip in next to him. He sinks underwater and I do too, opening my eyes to watch. His cheeks are full of air and he lets it out in a stream of bubbles, light blue, his face pale and reflective in the strange light. I reach out and hold on to his forearms.

"You!" he says quietly when we are back at the surface, breaking apart.

"You," I say back.

We wrap towels around our bodies and walk on to the sand, quickly, until the house recedes into the night. Near the rock pools at the end of the beach, Llew shakes out his own towel and lays it down for me. He indicates I should sit, and so I do. I am cold, stricken with adrenaline. He sits next to me, easily, puts his arm around me again. "Is this all right?" he asks.

Yes, it is all right. I try not to think of toxins leaving his mouth like a cloud, of what happens next. There is still time to stop it, but my curiosity has taken me too far now. I am pink with blood, best at the exercises, my body taller and stronger than my siblings. The careful marks on my thighs are a protection that surely, surely, could hold here for a little while. The water ahead of us is flat and infinite; shards of light through the sky like a dropped glass. He kisses the side of my head, his mouth landing on my wet hair, the top of my ear.

Why do I suddenly want to cry? Is it because in one fell swoop everything I've ever wanted has fallen upon me? I clutch for his knee, some kind of contact I have control over. I want to hold everything in the world in my arms, hold the universe itself.

Is this all right? is asked again, becomes a refrain. He is exaggeratedly gentle with me. It occurs to me I could also be a new thing, to be handled with wariness.

I think about the women and the things they described, the things I had not been supposed to hear, and about the muscles lengthening in my legs when I run, my body in motion, arms bending, torso arced. The startling joy of that movement, uncomplicated.

I am embarrassed about my dirty fingernails, the tough heels of my feet. In the end though, in the dark and the wet salt air, it doesn't matter.

My first thought in the silence afterwards is **I have survived.** Victory both small and large. My appetite for touch is whetted, but he has rolled on to his back in the sand and taken his hands off me.

When or if the men arrived, King implied it would mean our home burned to the ground, our blood spilled out on the shore, diluting in the water of the pool. I decide that our parents, in their love and fear for us, must have been mistaken. They grew too old. Their hearts were withered. It was not their fault. Compassion loosens in me as if I suddenly understand everything, benevolent, as if nothing bad could ever happen again.

Yet, back in my own bathroom, it turns out that the white cotton of my underwear is bloodied, and for a few minutes I am afraid that I am dying after all. It seems out of proportion to the pain, which is small but ignorable. There is nobody I can tell or ask, so I run through other symptoms in my head, examine the skin on the backs of my hands, the jelly of my eyes. Where he put his hands—collarbone, the tops of my arms, my cheek, briefly, though I could not meet his eyes—is unmarked. The bleeding soon stops and I tentatively declare myself safe for the moment, even if I am pale in the mirror.

Now I have intimacy, now intimacy is gone again, a damp weight of absence. And suddenly I am lonelier than ever before, a sharp hurt worse than actual pain. I replay the event in my head. I am thinking of every single act of his body, how even in the pain there was something needful and familiar, a slow piecing of myself together. My analysis is lacking; there are too many gaps. For a second I think about asking my sisters. But then I realize, with a deep and exhilarating terror, that I have gone beyond them here. I have a knowledge that they do not.

One thing I know for certain is that he is stronger than he has let on so far, a lot stronger than me. I was the strongest before, in that small window between King's death and Llew's arrival, the holiday without men. For a second, I am bereft.

It is only when I leave the bathroom and move to my bed that I discover something terrible is happening to Grace. Through the wall, the dying noises of an animal, a bird caught in the canopy. For a second I am afraid to go and see what the matter is, but then I remember that she is my sister, that her life is my life, and even though her door is closed and we allow each other those small privacies, guard them because Mother thinks them irrelevant, I push until it opens. My sister is sitting on the floor, leaning against the bed, her body folded in on itself. The bedding is soaked, streaked with bright red. The baby is coming. She bares her teeth at me, and I know to run.

The whole time I am sprinting down the corridors towards Mother I am conscious of Grace's pain, that white vortex of it binding me to her, and somewhere there is joy that she can't be rid of me so easily, that our sisterhood goes deeper than anything she can control. Llew is forgotten, the solid and sleek lines of him nothing against my unrecognizable sister, an animal now, on the ground. I clench my nails into my palms to feel my own pain, as if through that I could understand her better. There is no going close to it, even I know that, but I'm trying. When I inspect my palms I have left moon-shaped hooks in my skin, and I am thankful.

Every day I walked past him and every day he shouted at me across the traffic and every day I wilted under it. Headphones and scarf wound over my ears. He made his shouts louder. He came right up to me so I could lip-read. I fantasized about killing him daily. It felt incredibly good.

MOTHER HAS BEEN preparing. Buckets for hot water, armfuls of sheets and towels. New prayers and new words, **bassinet** and **postpartum**. When I shake her awake, she doesn't need the emergency explained. I help her carry the towels, the pillows, a pair of scissors and a penknife to Grace's room. We knock on Sky's door. We do not tell the men, and we lock Grace's door from the inside.

"The baby," Grace tells me, as if nobody else is around. "I had dreams about the baby. That it was a boy. And worse." The pain moves through her visibly, like a current. "I dreamed the baby had no mouth," she tells me. "I dreamed we buried him in the forest."

"Less of that," Mother says, as if she has seen it all before, and maybe she has. "When you're holding your daughter you'll forget everything."

Daughter, daughter, daughter. She is coming from a long way off, bathed in light. We are impatient to meet her.

"Help me," Mother commands. "We need to turn Grace."

We immediately put our hands and arms out to take her weight. I think of all the times we prayed to the sea, how those times were practice for disaster, and how much her heavy body feels like that disaster we have awaited.

Mother ties up her hair. There is a thumbprint of blood in the hollow of her neck.

The contractions are plentiful now, and they make Grace's body do things she hasn't given it permission to. Her limbs judder as she looks at me.

"I hope I die," she tells me, and then she makes eye contact with Mother. "I hope I finally fucking die."

"Less of that," Mother says once more, her hands merciless. Grace shuts her eyes, water moving down her face.

And then the night has fallen properly and here it is, after one last outburst from Grace, her voice a ragged howl: a thing covered in blood, soundless, on a long rope. Mother touches its mouth. She sponges the blood from the frog-like body, and underneath the skin is blue in the lamplight. Grace lies there, panting, limp.

Mother lowers her mouth to the baby's face, tries to blow air into its lungs. It's not long before she gives up. She takes the scissors and cuts the string, wraps the baby in a blanket, puts her into my arms.

"Can I see her?" Grace asks. Mother nods at me and I take the small body over to the top of the bed. Grace looks and then turns her head to the side, tears leaking from her eyes.

"Take it away," she says.

Before today, Sky was the only baby I had known. Raw as a shrimp, and loud. She put her hands inside our mouths, scratched at our gums with her small fingernails, wanted to see and know everything. Even when she grew long-limbed and sentient, when her own thoughts came out of her mouth like a shock to her as much as to ourselves, we could not lose that knowledge of her as an infant, that first impression. Grace had come to me fully formed, or rather I had come to her, any distance needing to be established, fought for. Sky was different. It is hard to deny her anything, wanting as we do to keep her small and safe, knowing that she is entirely of this world, that Mother and Grace and even my own tiny body, rocking inside Mother's, did not escape the other one completely. Sky's blood is irreproachable, essentially toxin-free, whole.

Sky and I go into the darkened bathroom, carrying the motionless baby before us. I close the door behind and we sit on the cold tiles while I try to think what to do. My hand tracks blood on the door, on the light switch. Sky rests on the edge of the bathtub as I wash the baby in the sink. She has been quiet, obedient, throughout the whole thing, making herself useful. She watches me, expressionless, as I unwrap the blanket stealthily, half-expecting to find fins. What I find is almost worse: it is a boy, even though Mother said that would be impossible. I wrap the baby back up, tighter still, before Sky can see.

This baby has no name. It is unlucky to pick names before the birth, Mother had told us. Unlucky to place that weight on such a small thing.

"Let me hold it," Sky asks. I worry about upsetting her, but when I pass the bundle over, very gently, she kisses its small face with no hesitation. Together we smooth down the hair of its head, still wet.

On the other side of the door, we hear Grace's voice rising up, a cry out, and then quiet. We wait to be told the coast is clear. It takes a long time and my arms hurt, but I don't put the baby down until Mother opens the door and holds out her arms for it and tells us to come in. Grace is sleeping. We move past the shape of her in the gloom, just one lamp in the corner to see by, sheets over her head, into the corridor. Mother closes the door behind us without saying another thing. The men, wherever they are, know not to make any sound.

The second we reach my room I insist Sky gets into the tub, sitting down with her and spraying the water over our skin and hair as hard as I can wrench the tap. Sky turns away from me as I rinse her long hair and rub a palmful of suds into it. When we are clean enough she curls herself at the bottom of my bed, asleep almost immediately. The ceiling above us is high and open, the air stale. I watch her for a while as the sky outside starts to lighten once more and the halo of water from her wet hair spreads outwards, revealing the tracery of the mattress underneath.

One day I looked at my husband and I thought, Would you knock them down? Would you stand up with your arms raised if they came for me? Coming for me was a thing I considered often, though the "they" was hazy, it changed all the time. Once I had thought this bad thought, I couldn't stop thinking about it. I thought it when he was asleep and I was awake. No, I realized one day. He would lie down and let them.

MOTHER OPENS MY door without knocking in the early morning, her face ruinous with exhaustion. She meets my eyes, silently motions for me to join her in the corridor. Her hand comes out to touch my face, just for a second. I can see myself in her, the bird-like plane of her cheekbones. "How much do you love your sister?" she asks, and when I outstretch my hands wide to indicate **this much,** she nods. She leans into my ear and asks me, quietly, to do something for her.

First I splash my face with cold water in the bathroom's grey light.

"Why was it a boy?" I ask her, made brave by her request.

She says that it wasn't. No ambiguity. And so that is it.

I carry the baby close to me, through our home and out on to the beach, afraid to unwrap the bloodstained cloth. Despite my frantic washing I can sense that there is still blood on me too—I can smell it, I can feel it—and I am afraid that one day there will be a stain we can't get out, and that will be it for us, the marking of the end. I am afraid somewhere in myself of the sweat belonging to Llew that I let dry on me, toxic dirt I have not washed off me yet, and I realize that this is the first time I've thought of him in hours.

Please let me live a clean and blameless life. Please let nothing touch me again, except for him, for without him I will surely die, is the prayer I say as I carry the baby away from our home for ever.

It is important to concentrate on anything but the coldness at the heart of the blankets, hardly bigger than the glass paperweight I salvaged from an empty room once.

I place the wrapped-up baby at the bottom of the boat. It isn't hot yet, there is crisp dawn fog where the horizon meets the sea, but I row hard. Normally I would be afraid, but there is no room for that now. My body still aches from last night. I know that disaster can take place despite everything, that there are no guarantees. The sweat drips into my eyes so that the light refracts, and for a second the world explodes around me, and I welcome it. I go as close to the line of buoys as I dare, the water utterly still, and I cradle the baby one last time.

"I'm giving him back to you," I tell the sea. There is no answer as I lower my arms into the water up to the elbow. The small parcel falls down through the water. Burial at sea. The only honourable option.

Halfway back to shore I judge it safe to stop for a second, and there I draw in the oars and cry harder than I have ever cried before. Harder than after the first razor-shell cut, than the time I fractured my ankle in a fall, than the time I fell asleep in the sun for hours and sunburn burst my skin open and Mother poured salt water over it to stop infection taking hold in my body. I press my hands to my eyes and make a noise that scares me, curl myself up to make the grief more manageable. Our home looms from the shore, and for the first time in a long time, maybe the first time in my life, I do not want to return. But I think about the rest of my family, waiting for me. I think about Llew; maybe he is waiting too. And so I do return.

. . .

After lunch, Grace is recovered enough to come down to the lounge, my hand hovering at her elbow as we walk the corridors together. Afternoon light unspools around our feet. The men are there too, the three of them slumped in chairs. They have discarded glasses half full of water on the side tables that must carry traces of their saliva and sweat, shoes kicked off where they sit, shoes and clothes that belonged to King.

"How are you feeling?" James asks, sombre. He gets up and puts a hand out to Grace, who takes it eventually. He places his other hand on top of hers. "We were so sorry to hear the news."

"I'm feeling bad," Grace tells him. She will not play along.

"Well," James says. "That's natural."

I stand next to the window, open it wider. Grace brings over a chessboard and we set it up on a table where we can feel the breeze. Gwil watches us, his eyes quick and alert, as if expecting us to make some violent movement. For a second I do want to throw the chessboard on to the floor, a hard laugh threatening to come up through my throat. Llew sits there, sensing something, and reaches out a hand to his son. "Come here, Gwil," he says. "You're in the way." He pulls him into a quick, one-armed embrace, then lets him go.

"We made coffee," James says. "Have some."

I pour a cup for the two of us to share from the cooling cafetière, sugaring it thickly. Grace drinks without complaint. James stares out at the sea, while Llew pulls up a chair to our chess game so he can watch. Gwil joins him but loses interest quickly, gets down on his hands and knees behind the sofa.

"Move your rook," Llew stage-whispers behind his hand as I stare, paralysed by his nearness, at the pieces.

"That's not fair," Grace says. "No cheating."

"I'll help you when it's your turn," he tells her.

"I don't want your help," she replies.

I don't move the rook. I see that there is more ground to be gained if I move the knight, so I do, toppling the board into check.

"Would you look at that," Llew says. He is still smiling. I turn away and stare at the sea, trying to find the point where I let the baby go. The supple water is forever changing. It's almost like it never happened, which gives me hope that one day it will be like it never happened.

Mother comes for me and Grace, Sky already with her. The men watch us go but do not follow. In the blue-washed afternoon we do our stretches, bending at the waist and sweeping our fingertips to the grass. Grace sits on a bench at the side, under the magnolia tree.

Mother tells us all to lie down on the ground, even Grace. Damp earth. She tells us to close our eyes. She puts a heavy sheet over each one of us, covering us head to toe. A new thing.

"For your grief," she tells us. "You can cry underneath that. Five minutes."

So we do.

Afterwards I nap in my room, exhausted. And it is when I draw back my curtains, deep sleep still gumming my eyes and the sky still light, that out on the sea, between the waves, I see a floating thing that doesn't belong to us.

On my knees at my bedside drawer, I pull out everything until I find my binoculars and then I run up the stairs and along the top corridor, until I reach the door to the terrace. My hands slip on the catch but finally I am out there, and I go straight to the railing, leaning over as far as I dare, worried it will sink before I can see it properly.

Ghost. I look at it through the binoculars, and I am almost doubled over with nausea immediately. I'm glad it's so far away. There is no way it could reach us. It's too large to be the ghost of the baby, bobbing and sick with its movements. I can't look at it for long, magnified or otherwise—no longer recognizably human but more dangerous, something to wash up on our shores swollen and racked with disease.

Still, I am not the expert in these things. I run to Grace's room, where she is napping too. She is still too pale, drained of blood, but I shake her awake anyway and I say, "A ghost, out on the sea," and she sits up as if she has been expecting it.

"I knew it," she says, her voice distant. "I knew this would happen."

As we walk past Mother's room, we hear breathing. She is in there with Sky, the two of them asleep on the bed, Mother lying facedown on her folded arms.

"Don't wake her," Grace instructs me. "She can't see this." At times like these I am reminded never to doubt my sister.

We return to the terrace, but it has gone. I pull her downstairs and out to the shore, right out on the jetty, checking the water spread out before us just in case. It is nowhere to be seen.

"Ghosts are fragile," Grace tells me after we have been looking for some time, passing the binoculars between us. "I believe that it happened."

I am grateful.

The sun is setting properly now, long and watery clouds falling violet to the horizon. We walk back to the pool and I take off my dress, slide into the water in my swimming costume. Grace sits on the side, watching me tread water for a while, illuminated in the centre of the pool. Birds call, long and low, from the forest behind her. I close my eyes against the perfect air on my face.

"When was the last time you played the drowning game?" I ask her.

"I didn't do it the whole time I was pregnant," she tells me. "I didn't want to hurt the baby." Her mouth becomes a hard line. Made brave with the love I am not used to, I wade to the side and put my arm around her shoulders, and this time she doesn't push me away.

"I'm sorry for what you had to do," she tells me.

"I didn't mind," I tell her. "I did it because I love you."

She nods. "You're a good sister."

Grace lies down on the tiles and closes her eyes as I scoop shallow handfuls of water over her head to cool her down. After a short while Mother comes out to sit next to the water, Sky trailing her.

"Well, would you look at this scene?" she announces brightly, sitting on the edge of a recliner. Sky takes off her own dress and jumps into the water to my left, and the resulting wave narrowly misses Mother.

"Isn't this lovely?" Mother says. "Isn't this just like the old days?"

I duck below the water, make a lattice with my hands that Sky can step on to. I lift her up into the air, her legs shaking with the effort of balancing. She is delighted. Soon she tips forward on to me and we both collapse under the water, laughing hard, clapping as we resurface. There is a pain in my side. For a second my joy is robust, there is no killing it.

Why tell anyone else about the ghost? Why ruin the evening, the smiles wide and painful on our faces? Mother settles back into her chair, crosses her legs at the ankle. She is once again the queen of everything she surveys.

We moved in a petal formation, groups of us. Sometimes we wore earplugs. For activities like running we went two by two and stayed alert. But still my women were harmed. We passed along details of the harm across the phone lines and we wept.

THE VERY NEXT DAY when we wake, we find our mother gone.

Sky is the one to discover Mother absent from the kitchen, from the garden, from the lounge. She lets out a great wail, calling our names until we run in with our hands up and our minds automatically listing the nearest weapons, the heavy objects, the best way to roll the bone of your knee into a person's stomach or nose.

Person, not woman. New kinds of defensiveness come to us as we run, words and images swimming up through our minds as though they were there, latent in us all along, waiting for something to call them—the musk of Llew's armpit, the visible veins of James's forearm, even Gwil's flat, pale child's body walking back and forth through the garden—and here we are with our own new violence, which we do not need and cannot use. All we can do is comfort Sky, hold her shaking body so tightly that we cannot feel our own shaking.

We picture Mother in white. We picture her with cloth in her mouth and bundled at her extremities, more than King had needed, much more. We picture her out on the last slip of sea before she moves beyond sight in the pre-dawn, looking back to the house in the mist, her daughters treacherously asleep.

We think it might be a test, not unlike the other acts of endurance we have undergone through our lives, so we walk around the house, calling until our voices are gone. Opening cupboards that have been closed for years, finding nothing but old brooms and the acrid smell of mice. Peering inside the chest freezer and the fridge, both large enough to hold a woman. Hauling open the coal cellar, a small hatched enclosure around the back of the house, though the leftover dust and darkness make us shudder. Nothing.

"We did see your mother, earlier," Llew tells us down by the pool, where we find him doing press-ups by the side of the water. I am thrilled, secretly, to see him move, to catalogue it alongside his other movements. He stops when we are next to him, stands and looks down at us, panting slightly. His hair is sticking up, his eyes tired. "She set off before dawn, knocked on our door on the way. She didn't want to disturb you."

"You should have woken us," Grace says. "She never goes to the mainland. Never. It was always King." King, whose body could withstand whatever atmospheric poisons we keep in check here.

"We didn't do the breathing exercises," Sky says, but Llew just shrugs.

"I just know that she took the motorboat," he tells us.

We go down to the shore and, sure enough, only the rowing boat is left.

"Why didn't you go? Or James?" Grace asks. "You would be faster."

"You really want us gone, don't you?" says Llew, unbothered. "Well, I don't want to leave Gwil yet. He's still weak. Besides, our people are coming for us, and it's best for us to stay tight, for now. We agreed it all with her."

We look at the lone boat where it is moored up, tiny in the distance.

"Your mother," he says, chuckling a little,

shaking his head. "She's an admirable woman. I think you're underestimating her."

"So you're friends now?" Grace asks, hard-faced. "Why would she leave us with you?"

"She should have told us," Sky says, kicking a pebble down the beach, and then another.

Llew throws up his hands. "Well," he says, glancing at me. "You're the ladies of the house for now. I suppose that means you're in charge of the rules."

"We should carry on as normal," Grace says. "She could come back at any time."

Llew gazes out to sea, his hand cupped against the light. "You're grown-ups now," he says, turning back to us. "Do what you want."

Back in the dining room we sit at our usual places, taking things in. Sky rearranges the cutlery into geometric patterns. Grace looks out through the window to the empty beach and does not tell Sky to stop.

"A break from Mother," Grace says eventually, and she starts to laugh, because hasn't this been our undared-for dream, us sisters together? Sky and I join in, hysterical. Once we calm ourselves we eat yesterday's bread spread with the last honey, a crystal mess at the bottom of the jar. The men come in just as we are finishing and we lift our hands to them. James is gripping Gwil's shoulders. They are all in a good mood. Llew meets my eye, winks.

I should search further for Mother with my sisters, but the opportunity to be alone with Llew is too good to miss. Some excuse, any excuse. **She could arrive home at any time,** I tell myself, **it is not yet an emergency,** and even through my elation I am angry at her for leaving without telling us. Llew is not in the lounge, the swimming pool, the forest. Eventually I find him on the old tennis court, hitting mouldy balls against mesh grown soft with rain and age. He does not jump when I step inside his field of vision, but instead reaches down for a racquet and throws it to me without missing a beat. We play for a short time in the sticky heat, my body feeling heavy, deliberate. Soon he looks at me, then puts his own racquet on the floor. "Let's go inside," he says. He rests a hand lightly where my spine meets my neck, the fragile knot of bone.

In my room, the air under the high ceiling

charged with dust, he tries to talk to me about why we are here, but when I explain that we are just keeping ourselves safe, in retreat from the danger that extends to the very atmosphere itself, he goes quiet. **Stop talking, Lia.** I have said too much. Instead we kick off the blankets to the floor, the satin coverlet with the fussy embroidery, shining bumps meant to emulate flowers. We take off our clothes in the afternoon heat.

When he has finished touching me, we share more about ourselves. He is more talkative than I have ever seen him, and I am overjoyed. Everything I hear, I try to match. I arrange myself into it with ease.

"What do you like?" I ask him.

Tomatoes, green fruits, the ocean in the morning, he says.

"I don't like mussels," I say, a scoping, a sounding. The shrivelled purse of them, like the dead hearts of birds or frogs.

"Oh, but I love them," he tells me.

Slight panic in my chest. "I don't hate them," I retract. "But there are other things I would rather eat."

I go into my bathroom for a glass of water, take a little time away from him in the spirit of caution, the spirit of being a responsible woman, sticking my face out of the window to reach air he hasn't breathed. I am taking too long. I panic that he will go, bored of me and my words, other things to attend to. But when I open the door he is still there. The cover is pulled up to his waist and he looks, in the gloom, as if he has been cut in half.

I debate the sort of small accident I could orchestrate that would keep him close to me. Broken foot, maybe. I could drop a glass bottle, have him step on the shards. I consider the solid lines of his form. No, his is the type of body that heals almost immediately, otherwise known as a man's body.

"What's the worst thing that's ever happened to you?" I ask. I think again about that rabbit under King's foot, the salted earth in my mouth and nostrils.

"My father died," he says. "Like yours. Years and years ago. Gwil had only just been born."

"What's the worst thing you've ever done?" I ask next.

"No, you first," he says, so I tell him about the baby. His eyes widen in alarm. He tells me it was not my fault, then repeats it.

"Have you ever killed anyone?" I ask him, after. **Be worse than me.**

"Everyone's killed someone," he tells me. But I have not.

"You would love the mainland," Llew says after a period of silence. "I think you really would love it." He sits up and looks around: the ugliness of the wallpaper, faded with age and sunlight; the plush of my bed's padded headboard, a sickly pink. "This isn't a place for young women. You're not the type to be shut away."

"I could come with you," I say.

He smiles. "You could. That would be good, wouldn't it?" He reaches out to my face.

Love might be able to protect me there the way it has protected me here. Love could form itself into a barrier against my tongue and airways like the mouthguard King brought back for Grace to stop her body from grinding her teeth down, the susurration of her jaw a night-time sound to join the sea. New loves, new protections, new forms of life-guarding. I don't know what this love is capable of, but as I study his face—angles, the soft curl of lips, his eyes closed now—I believe it could do anything.

. . .

In the garden, alone, I pull up white flowers with my hands, cutting the stems with my fingernails. Sap spills out and stains my skin a yellowish green. I shred the petals, turn over on to my back, cross my hands across my heart and pretend that I am dead for a few seconds. The sun burns on my eyelids.

Through the euphoria, I remind myself to be cautious. I know that I have the emotionality of women on the land. If I were there, it would draw men to me like a beacon. It's important to keep this from Llew, so that he knows I am a person he can love, not a person he will feel compelled to hurt. These are the kinds of things that Mother and King taught us about love outside the borders.

Somewhere distant in my mind, I know I should be doing something. Taking the rowing boat as far as it could take me, bailing out water all the way, and under the strain of the air watching through binoculars for the outline of Mother returning to us. I got her as my loved-most this year. That gives me some sort of responsibility. But I do not go.

Instead I move to the pool, where Sky and Grace lie on recliners angled specifically to get the best view out to sea, heads touching, arms linked. Their faces ask **Where have you been?** but I refuse to feel guilty. The men and Gwil are grouped around the other end of the pool. They seem to be talking seriously, so I don't want to interrupt them, but Llew looks over to me and he waves, calls out my name. I wave back. He watches me walk over to a mint-striped recliner near my sisters, picking the one that is cleanest, hitching my pale skirt up over my knees. It is easy to slip my sunglasses on to my face and the straps down my shoulders and to settle back, to feel his gaze on me like water, like a thing I deserve.

It's not long before we become too hot lying there under the midsummer sun but we don't move, we are languid and paralysed after the morning's shock. Even at the approach of evening the air is stagnant; deep purple clouds gather and still the heat has not broken. We stay out until the first fat drops of rain hit us and then we run inside together. Standing in the lounge with our faces flushed, my sisters pull their dresses on over their swimsuits as the men watch. Grace's stomach is soft and round where the baby stretched her body.

The men offer to make dinner. Grace is reluctant but eventually she agrees. When the rain eases, they send Gwil out to fetch oysters and shellfish, and through the open windows we hear him whooping as he runs down the beach. The three of us retreat to Grace's room automatically, like we have done so many times before, sprawling over her bed, but almost immediately she sits up, restless, something occurring to her.

"Let's go to Mother's room," she suggests. "It's nicer."

We reexamine our mother's clothes in the cupboard, smelling of antiseptic and the lavender she takes from the garden. Then we turn to the cabinet in her bathroom, the brown bottles of medicines, the pills in white cardboard boxes with red lettering. **Tramadol. Olanzapine. Diazepam.** Grace reads them out with a grimace, with a flourish. The words mean nothing to us. The three of us check under the bed, making Sky stick her arm into the shadows. She draws back a sleeve of dust. We count the pairs of underwear in Mother's drawers and open her bedside cabinet to find a pair of tweezers, the dead stub of a votive candle, nothing more.

"When will she come back?" Sky asks when we have finished our inspections and laid ourselves on the bed in a row.

"I don't know," I say, staring up at the ceiling, the clouded lamp in its bronze fitting.

"Soon," Grace assures her. "Soon."

The rain returns, grows worse. The energy builds in my chest. My sisters fall asleep in the faltering light. When I know they won't wake, I get up and walk down the corridor to my own bedroom, my own bathroom. I left the window open and rainwater has sluiced the tiled floors, the walls. When I close it, I see the waves are bigger than usual. Their saline residue will be on the windows of the lounge, the dining room's glass doors. One day they will overwhelm us, water moulding our carpets and warping the parquet, leaving tidemarks on the wallpaper. But I hope to be long gone by then.

It's too stormy for the drowning game but my feelings will not wait, my body is aching to be submerged, so I turn on the taps, stripping off my clothes as the water runs. I test the temperature, wanting it tepid, somewhere between the air and the sea. When the tub is full enough I climb in, lean back and go under in one sharp movement. Below the surface, the sound of the storm cuts out.

Loneliness must have changed my body over the years. I think about my heart blown out of shape and unfit for the job, made of the knotted purple veins that river Mother's calves. Dark water in the channels of my brain, a stiffness in my hands. My lungs, red and wet, the air pressed out of them.

Soon I run out of breath. My thoughts become a flat line of light. I wait a second past the point where I know I can't stand it any more and then I burst up through the water gasping—and I have survived again, I have survived, and my heart is singing and my eyes are dark and the wind outside seems quieter, drowned out by the pitch of my own blood in my ears.

I stay in the now-cold bath for some time, rejoining my sisters once I feel ready. They are still asleep. The indigo circles under Grace's eyes are back, and Sky is pallid too now. Something is wrong with us, something has always been wrong with us. I find the space I am allowed and move back into it. Either side of me, my sisters murmur before lapsing back into sleep. I breathe shallowly, pain under my rib cage, hair wet. I wait for Mother's return with great patience, but she hasn't arrived by the time I hear the men calling us in chorus for dinner, two low voices and Gwil raising his own reedy voice for the first time, as if he is not so weak any more. I wake my sisters and we walk together through the quiet of the house, where I can pretend we are one, before we step into the lighted space of the dining room.

One last flare of joy, after dinner, before I go to sleep. A small bunch of flowers from the garden on my pillow. Violet and yellow, the petals growing limp already. I want to keep them but make myself press them down into my bin and hide them with a drift of tissue paper, for secrecy's sake, for safety.

I mourned him gracefully for three months, before a postcard arrived. It had a woman dressed in a frilled dress on the front, tomato-red. I'm alive, don't worry about me, **it said on the back. My hands started to violently shake so I disposed of the poisonous object in the incinerator at once, taking care not to breathe in the smoke.**

THE SECOND DAY without Mother, the shore is strewn with incredible amounts of flotsam. Rope and seaweed. Large rocks and small, the sand partly washed away. The three of us pick through it, looking for anything valuable. We retreat only when Sky finds a milky jellyfish, which we think for a terrible moment is a ghost or part of one, and reminds us that without Mother's presence we are endangering ourselves in every waking moment of the day. We shake a little once we find a part of the beach that feels safe, and cry a little too, putting our hands on each other's shoulders, my sisters even touching mine.

"Let's go to the perimeter," Grace says when we have recovered, sitting cross-legged on the sand. She picks up a pebble near her foot and aims it at the water, but it falls just short. "Maybe there is someone who will help."

Who? I don't ask, but we go with her. She picks up more pebbles and puts them in her pocket. In the forest we step very carefully through the foliage. At the border, before we can stop her, Grace throws the pebble as hard as she can past the barbed wire.

"Is there anyone out there?" she shouts. I put both my hands on her mouth and she resists, pulls us both down to the floor. Sky shields her head, but nothing happens. No movement in the leaves, the trees.

"Why would you do that?" I say to her once we have stood up, breathing hard.

She shakes her head. "You love them. You love the men."

Outrage. I put her in a headlock. We blunder too close to the wire, face certain death, and only then do we stop.

"How dare you touch me," my sister says, and her voice is poison.

The three of us sit down on the leaf-strewn dirt. I catch my breath, stare at Grace. After a short time she reaches into her pocket and draws out a roll of white cloth, part of an old sheet. She passes one end to me, unwinds it and gives the other end to Sky, and we hold it taut as she rips it into smaller rags with her knife. She ties them to branches and even, daringly, one to the border itself, a part less rusted than the rest. So Mother can find her way back, she explains. Or so allies, other women, can swell our ranks. Because surely they are out there, somewhere.

"We should have done this earlier," Grace says as she ties the knots. "We should have done this when King died."

Sky shivers. Mother does not use the word **died.** Only **gone.** Grace spots this.

"Died, died, died!" she says. "Say it, Sky. Go on. King is dead."

"King is dead," Sky says, doubtfully. She picks up a stick and draws a line in the dirt.

"That wasn't so difficult, was it?" Grace says. She ties the last scrap of fabric and surveys her handiwork.

We move to the terrace to establish a watch for Mother. I monitor the sea through binoculars until my vision fizzes at the edges and I have to lie down with my palms pressed over my eyes. Another sister takes up the watch instead. We pass the time like that for a while.

Sometime in the afternoon I hear music coming from the ballroom, faint, and ask to be excused. Grace moves her shoulders almost imperceptibly. "Suit yourself," she says. Her eyes are trained elsewhere.

Llew is playing something mournful this time. He turns and smiles when I enter, pauses with his hands still on the keys.

"I was hoping you would hear," he says.

He stands up, closes the lid of the piano and walks over to me, putting his hands either side of my face in the way I am getting used to.

This time when we are in my room I pull at his left ear with my nails, testing a reaction. I bite neatly with my jaw. It doesn't make him angry, but there's a slight extra pressure in the weight of his body. I am seeking places of weakness, just in case. "Hey," he says eventually, indulgently. "You're hurting me."

Good, I think.

He touches my hair. My heart swells like a broken hand to twice its size, the same sort of tenderness.

Love only your sisters.

When Llew leaves me, I go to Mother's room and sit on her bed for a while, staring at the irons. It is the chore of the one without love to keep them shining, free of dust. I haven't been doing it often enough. Mother keeps a tin of polish, a cloth, in her dressing table. I take them out and get to work.

I don't bother spending much time on King's. The living need the love more: I can make my own judgements here. When it comes to Mother's, though, I take extra care, picturing her out there on the ocean with water in the boat's floor, her body bent over as the air assaults her like a wave. Two days.

Invocation for good health for our mother.

I touch every one of the irons like a dare before I leave the room.

Maybe Mother will just stay away for a while. Maybe the way I am feeling will wear off, a dream or an ache, powerful only because I am not used to getting what I want. It's possible that by the time she returns I could be myself again. If I am good.

So I take my own temperature, score vigorously at my ankles in a warm bath. I have survived this long alone, haven't I. But my starved feelings, tamed into listlessness, still flower up in my chest.

New prayer: **Let me grow tired of this.**

Please, I think, my pulse nervous and rebounding. **Soon**.

There is a blood moon. I walk to the end of the jetty and lie there against the wooden boards to watch it. I want to be alone with it, the orb seeming close enough to touch. The ponderous water below my head hushes my ears. I feel sick with the number of symbols we are swimming against, with how porous the borders of sky and sea and land feel all at once.

This is a time to be with my sisters and I know I should fetch them, draw them by the hands and bring them to watch, so we can sit silent on the planks and think about what is coming. I want only to be alone but in the end they come anyway; the white shapes of them moving along the jetty to me, heavy cotton shawls wrapped around their bare shoulders. They lay themselves down next to me without speaking and I go to sit up, but Sky catches my arm. "Stay," they ask me, one after the other. "Please." Soft and knowable once more. They can switch it on and off at will.

We look up towards the sky, reach up our arms and our hands, and we pray the way that Mother taught. The air is dusky around us.

We almost don't hear James approach, but the creak of the boards behind us gives him away, makes us sit up. Watery eyes, sallow skin. I've looked at Llew so much that looking at James is a disappointment. I wonder if he sees me and my sisters as distinct or as three branches of the same tree, indistinguishable apart from slight variations in height, in the curl and hue of our dark hair, backlit by red.

"Do you know why the moon is like that?" he asks us. His voice is hoarse, nervous. He clears his throat.

"It's a blood moon," Grace says.

"It's just dust," James tells her. "Dust in the atmosphere." We don't reply. He fidgets with an item around his neck.

"What's that?" asks Sky.

"This?" says James, pulling it out. He holds it up towards us. "It's a rosary." A silver cross on beads.

"What's it for?" she asks again.

"For praying," James says. "For protection. You girls pray, don't you?" He smiles quickly, uncertain.

"We do," says Grace.

"We could all pray now. Together," he says. "If you like."

"No, thanks," I say.

"No," says Grace. "But you can stay here for a while with us."

We shuffle up to make room for him. James seems uncomfortable. We fix our eyes upon him. For once, we have the upper hand definitively. I can feel it in my chest. We could do things to hurt him. He might not fight back; he might not know how to protect himself against us. Some of the higher waves send a gentle spray up on to our skin.

"Is Mother back yet?" Sky asks him.

"No," James tells her. "It's just a matter of time, though. She'll arrive tomorrow, I expect."

Sky slumps against Grace, disappointed. Grace kisses her on the forehead, smooths back her hair.

"The journey can take a few days, with King." She pauses. "Took a few days. So it's all right. No cause for panic."

James nods.

We fall silent at the sight of a shooting star above us. I follow it with my eyes until it winks out of view, long past the point where it interests everyone else. One star among a million; a moon refracted in its own honey, plumed by dust. It is so far away, but I want to reach into the sky and pull it down regardless. I want to hold it in my hands, to break it apart and make it mine.

The closest I ever got to one of the damaged women was sitting in the sauna, a long time ago, back in the days when it still worked. I couldn't have been older than ten, eleven. It was rare to be left unsupervised with one of them. It could not have been an accident. She shuffled around, coughing. Like most of the women, her body seemed run-down, a creature unable to flourish. I watched her very carefully, the way I would have watched something that had limped out from the forest. I was over-warm, but she used her hands to scoop water on to the heated element with a shiver. My healthy child's body sweated with ease. Occasionally she let out a faint moan or cry. I pretended not to hear.

What must it be like, to live in a world that wants to kill you? Where every breath is an affront? I should have asked her that day about how it felt. Occasionally she still pressed muslin to her mouth, but there was no blood that I could see. Her painful eyes, when they fixed on me, made me nervous.

That evening, we all gathered in the ballroom. One of the other women had been deemed ready for the water cure, her body practised and open. King sat on a chair pushed to the wall, behind the piano, which made a physical barrier between him and the women. There were four or five of them, most of whom had stopped flinching at the sight of him, but he was chivalrous about keeping his distance.

Mother entered the room after the rest of us were all seated. She went straight to the woman and placed a hand on her shoulder, a signal for her to rise, and brought her to the front. The large curing basin waited there, full of water, the ever-present jar of salt on the floor next to it. Mother filled both hands with the salt and sprinkled it on the surface in a spiral pattern, her movements graceful. More saline and viscous than the sea, something closer to our own blood. The woman kneeled down with difficulty and the gathered fabric of her blue gown sighed. Mother clasped her hands and put them on the back of the woman's neck as she slowly pressed her face into the water. All the lamps along the wall were blazing.

Time passed and passed. The woman's body was compliant at first, but soon her own hands, pressed to the floor, began to twitch, then flail. She was trying to push herself up. The water rose over the sides of the basin as the woman struggled, soaking the front of Mother's dress. Mother did not react. We waited, our breath caught in our mouths. And then, as always, just past the point when we were sure it would be over, she was pulled up, strawberry-flushed and gasping. She reeled almost over to the floor, supported at the last minute by Mother's arms. Mother wrapped a small white towel around her shoulders, as tenderly as if she were one of my sisters.

The cured woman stood and the others got to their feet and clapped fervently. And we, the sisters at the back, clapped too. Our father just watched, still seated, understanding that the atmosphere did not belong to him. That edge of hysteria, the sense of being saved. The woman cried as she came back to her seat, the towel trailing in her hand. It could have been joy, or shock, or both. I wonder now if she felt the difference already. If somewhere within her there lived a kernel of new strength, and whether this strength would mark her out visibly on the mainland or whether she would just live with the knowledge of it inside her, perfect and luminous.

I knew so little at the time of what she had endured, that damaged woman, though I discovered it all much later from the Welcome Book. Why didn't the men do anything? I wondered, when I finally knew the truth. Why didn't they make things easier? But back then, watching her walk away from the curing water of the basin, I didn't know anything about power, or love, or taking what you can just because you can. Why should I, it wasn't something that had been laid out for me yet, it wasn't necessary information. "Sometimes it's better not to know," said Mother. At the time, that was good enough for me.

Stupid to meet a stranger but I was still convinced by the intrinsic goodness of people, I was so innocent, and I had not been exposed to the world very much. I didn't understand how rapidly things had changed, how all that had been needed was permission for everything to go to shit, and that permission had been granted. I didn't know that there was no longer any need for the men to hold their bodies in check or to carry on the lie that we mattered.

ON THE THIRD DAY without Mother I wake early. It is a very clear day, the promise of intense heat later. I stand on the terrace, breathing the salt air off the silent bay. Below me, something breaks the surface of the swimming pool. I move to the rail and see a figure in a long white gown—the drowning dress, I realize, with its weights and embroidery. She breaks the surface. It is Grace, her hair loose in dark ropes around her shoulders. I am too far away to see the expression on her face.

As I watch, she swims to the shallow end and takes in deep gulps of air, resting against the side for a few seconds. Then she goes back into the deeper water and holds herself under again. I count the seconds. She surfaces desperately. She pulls herself under again. It does not seem to be giving her the satisfaction that it gives me, no end point, no closure.

Her movements become more furious, not less. She is making up for lost time, maybe, her body once more her own, to use as she wants. I stop watching after the third time, ashamed. I let her do what she needs to do.

I am standing in the centre of the kitchen. Sea air comes in from the open door. The scent of citrus fruits, though we have not grown them for a while. The landscape stopped supporting them: thinning of the soil, vestigial minerals. We used to cut the oranges and lemons into medicinal segments. We would give them to the damaged women, to wedge in their mouths and hold there for a long while, letting the juice pour down their chins, their throats. Sometimes we did it to each other too.

Llew is a shadow against stainless steel, against the cracked white paint heavy with dust. He tucks both his arms around my waist, his chin resting on my head, having entered the room out of nowhere. I am being held and I am not used to holding. Nobody has seen us, and I can't tell if I want to be caught or not. It would be a disaster, yet at least someone would bear witness, would confirm that this is real, that this is happening to me. But he lets go at the sound of footsteps. Grace enters the kitchen and stops at the sight of us, but his hands are not on me now, there is still no proof. Love can be that slippery: the difference between touching and not-touching, fallible memory, my skin forgetting already. He raises his palms to her, puts his hands where she can see them. "Good morning to you both," he says, his first words of the day to her and to me.

I think a lot about what it could all mean. Significance hangs around him like a cloud. Every cough, every glance is telling me something. Hands, again. This time laid out on the breakfast table with white cotton cloth showing in the space between his fingers, sitting next to me as Grace ladles out fruit. His knee nudges mine; he lingers when everybody else has drifted back to the kitchen to wash up. It is not an accident. He takes me by the arm, pulls me up the stairs. "Come on," he says. He is overjoyed by my body. It's like he, too, has never seen one before.

New dangers, though, coming to the surface like the bubbles of soap. His breath has a copper bitterness. It fills the room as he sleeps for a few minutes in my bed, breathing hard through his mouth. I turn away from it. Again I want to hurt him, want to save his life or to ruin it, something, anything, I have not decided. I want him to leap for my approval like a fish, body twisting, and I want to be the one who dictates the terms, but when I try, small stabbing gestures towards intimacy, he doesn't react enough. He pulls my own hair over my mouth.

Afterwards we walk back down to the sea and I point to the horizon, and he goes in up to his ankles despite the danger. I am so close to going in after him, a lifetime of instinct already overridden. I hold firm, on the shore, watching for his body to be pulled under. But I don't kid myself. I am saved only because he is not asking me directly, not holding out his hand and imploring.

I lie on the men's side of the pool now. I have discovered that it's all right for me to be close to them, that my body feels no different really. My eyes do not redden. My ears do not bleed. But my sisters won't join me, even when I ask. Grace doesn't bother to answer; she just stares at me with a maddening half-smirk, then looks away. So I leave them out on the terrace and take my towel down to the pool, positioning a recliner between James and Llew. James includes me in his small jokes, which I do not understand, but I smile anyway.

Llew goes inside and returns with drinks on the enamel tray that Mother uses when we are sick or confined. It is some kind of alcohol mixed with juice from a tin. Sudden flashback: Mother and King clawing at each other in large love, small rage, like something from a half-remembered dream. I close my eyes for a second, gather my composure. The dream is the days which hang in front of me, smooth and opaque as a skin on hot milk. I do not want to think too clearly, to see too closely.

Llew touches my foot when James looks away. I lie on my front so that the sun can hit my back and both of them are watching me, I can tell, and the confirmation of my existence makes me self-conscious. James touches me too, on the arm, paternally. "You're our friend, aren't you?" he says. "Our little friend." His speech is slurred. I do not feel afraid of them.

Llew pulls at my hair when James slips into the water, wraps it around his hand. "Beautiful," he says into my ear. He bites my neck and I start laughing hysterically, so that James pauses and stands up, watches us with water streaming down his body, but doesn't say anything.

Previous long days at the pool, days with and without love. King pushing athletically through the water, length after length, skin burnishing even as we watched. We couldn't swim if he was swimming: he became impatient at how slow we were. I cried, sometimes, behind my sunglasses where nobody could see. The damaged women stayed inside, generally. They only really trusted the air in the early morning, the dusk, when it was easy to breathe.

When James goes inside for a glass of water, Llew puts out his hand to me, closes it around my forearm. The air is bone-dry, heat catching in my throat. He kisses me open-mouthed with his sunglasses still on, sunglasses I recognize as King's, then jumps into the pool. I follow him blindly. Under the sun-warmed water I turn somersaults, over and over and over. Llew holds me under by my legs and I do not struggle to get to the surface, I leave my body weightless and inert, thinking, **Do**

what you want do what you want do what you want.

There is a commotion at the surface as I lie suspended, joyful. Llew is thrashing at the water. He lifts me up in his arms and I respond immediately, wrapping my own around his neck, but when I break the surface he is panicked. James is standing on the side of the pool, staring.

"I thought there was something wrong," Llew shouts, letting go of me. "Why did you do that? I thought I had drowned you." He stands up in the water, leans over me. His voice becomes louder. "Do you know what that looked like? Was that some sort of joke?"

"I'm fine," I say. I forgot myself. It was peaceful, to be held under by him like that. Unchangeable stasis, the light filtering through.

"Calm down, Llew," James says. "There's no harm done, is there?"

Llew falls back, lets himself sink up to his neck in the water. "Don't ever pull a stunt like that again," he says to me.

"I'm sorry," I say to him, climbing out of the water. I do not like the new way he is looking at me, as if I have revealed something about myself it would have been better to keep hidden.

Before long, James falls asleep in the sun, his arm flung across his face to shade him. I watch the movement of his whistling breathing, his reddening skin.

"Let's go to the forest again," Llew says in a stage whisper. He has forgiven me and I am stupidly grateful. He throws one of my sandals at me and I almost catch it, almost fall over as I put it on. "Quickly!" He glances at James. "Before the old fucker wakes up."

As we walk down the pebbled ground towards the forest, I look back to search for Grace's face at a window, but I would not be able to see her anyway: the glass reflects the glare outwards and there are too many panes to count. She could be behind any one of them.

In the forest itself we head for the border until we are sure we can't be seen. We are uncomfortably close to it, for me at least, but I have to trust him to protect me, something that's getting easier all the time. Llew has brought his towel but the twigs and rocks stick through. I am on my hands and knees and I know that bruises will come up almost immediately, that I am thin-skinned and woundable, and somewhere within me I like this, the proof, the map of this new joy. It is hard to keep my balance, the alcohol affecting how the forest holds itself, how I hold myself.

Afterwards, I am very happy. The leaves of the forest murmur around us as though they are happy too. It is good to be in love, to have the whole world on your side. I lie on the towel as Llew walks around nearby, throwing rocks, inspecting leaves. Even in the shade, the breeze, the heat is almost unbearable. It is warmer since their arrival, I know I am not imagining it.

Llew lies down in the shadow next to me, and I move over, rest my head on his stomach. He touches my face absent-mindedly, putting his fingers briefly inside my mouth, cupping them under my chin. I bring up the outside world, and he asks me, bored, what I want to know, but I can't say out loud, **What did it feel like to have a child? Will you have more children? What was it like for you to be young? What does it feel like to have a man's life, and a man's body, that solid mass? What are other men like? What**

does it feel like to go beyond the border? Does the air stretch the skin of your face? Does it damage your body? Do you think about dying too?

"God, it's boiling," he says. I push myself up on my forearms, purse my lips and blow on to his face. He keeps his eyes shut, moves his lips faintly into a smile, and suddenly I am sick to my stomach.

"Anything," I say.

"Why do you care so much?" he asks.

"I just want to know," I say, and my eyes start to water.

"Are you crying?" he asks, without opening his eyes.

"No," I say. "I have a headache." I lie down so that the water won't course down my face. Old trick, learned so early I don't remember when. Perhaps it is a human trick, something I was born with.

"Don't cry," he says, finally looking at me properly. "I hate it when women cry. It's manipulative." He gets to his feet. "Go inside and take an aspirin," he says, pulling me up too.

"You want to watch that," he adds. "You want to take care of yourself better." He puts both hands on my shoulders and kisses me briefly on the forehead. And I wonder how much he knows about the effect his body could have on mine, whether he is taking his own precautions.

We are heading back to the house when we hear voices. Just my sisters, but they are making a commotion, the noise dipping and ebbing. Llew looks at me, unsure, but only for a second.

"They'll be playing a game," I say. We walk into the next clearing.

My sisters are standing in front of something, and they are jeering. It's darker here, the leaves bunched close together so the light cannot get through. Rocks coated in moss like tongues, leaves fruiting with mould. They don't hear our approach.

"Where is your mother?" Sky asks, her back still to us. "Where is she?" She reaches out and shakes a branch, carelessly. Birds crash out into the leaves above them.

"Why aren't your men looking after her?" Grace joins in. "Why aren't you?"

"You must have left her all alone," says Sky.

"What would she think if she knew?" says Grace.

Llew walks swiftly in front of them and my sisters start, fall back. He takes Gwil's arm. His face is tear-stained, trousers only half done up.

"What have you done to him?" he asks, voice dangerous. Grace stands her ground.

"Nothing," she says, chin up. "We just found him alone in the woods." She looks at Gwil. "Sneaking around, doing the things that men do."

Gwil turns away from them, hangs his head. He wipes his eyes with the back of his arm.

"You leave him alone," Llew says.

"Or else what?" Grace asks, smiling. But when he takes a step closer to her she moves away from him, despite her bravado.

"Being cruel to a child. It's terrible," he says. "If you were a man I would have hit you without thinking about it."

"Good thing I'm not, then," Grace says, and his hands rise, but then fall back to his sides.

My sisters and I leave the men among the trees. Both of them are jittery, euphoric. We have survived another thing. And what is a boy if not a hurtable man, a safe version? Something has been proved, something established.

But we are still fragile, and we are not allowed to forget this. In the evening I am woken from a nap by Grace pulling at my hair, slapping me around the face until I raise my hands, until I roll out of the bed, and when I look at her I see how red she is, how hysterical.

"Mother," she says breathlessly, stopping her assault for a second. "Mother!"

"What?" I ask her, forgetting about my ringing ears. "What's happened?"

"She's still gone!" Grace shouts at me.

Sky runs into the room, clawing at her face and keening until I find some muslin from my drawer and wrap it around her mouth, her throat. It does not still her voice.

It overtakes me then, the fear, and my knees buckle, and I start to scream too. Because suddenly it is real: Mother is gone.

"She's not coming back," Sky says hoarsely, and Grace slaps her hard—she never hits Sky, we are gentle with her, we are mindful of her—and so then I hit Grace to remind her she is no longer untouchable, she is no better than us. Grace looks at me, raises her hand to her face.

Then, at the doorway, presence felt before seen: the men. They come into the room and I instinctively make to push them out, but let my hands drop before I reach them. We need to stand out on the lawn and let our bodies fall to the ground, or be caught in each other's arms; we need to push ourselves under the water over and over again.

"Mother," gasps Sky, moving the muffler from where I have wrapped it, wet with her spit and tears. "Mother."

"Girls," says James. He looks taken aback by our force. "Please don't be like this. She'll be back soon. I know she will be. Maybe even tonight. She must have got caught up in the port. Or stayed for dinner."

"How do you know?" Grace shoots at him. "Why should we trust you?"

And he gives the only possible answer. "What choice do you have?"

My eyes are drawn as usual to Llew, who looks horrified to see us like this, enough to make me feel ashamed. He refuses to meet my eyes. Gwil is the only one not bothered by our hysterics. He is watching us with an expression of intense interest, with something approaching glee.

"It's the same thing over and over," Sky says, and she is sobbing openly now. "You keep saying the same things, but where is Mother? When will she be back?" She sits on the floor without warning, as if her knees have given way.

"Please," says James, as if we were hurting him. "Come downstairs with us. Let us look after you." He moves to comfort Sky, but she shuffles away from him on her hands and knees, leaves him standing with his arms outstretched.

"Right, enough of this," Llew says. He claps, then looks at us expectantly. "Come on."

The fight has gone out of us. After some hesitation, Sky stands up. We follow the men down the stairs, holding hands, united in defeat.

The dining room is a mess, cookbooks and plates, empty bottles and packets strewn around. The men do not live lightly on our territory. I look sideways at Grace, but she doesn't seem to notice. My hands itch to gather everything into piles, to tip it into the sink and get the water running, but I don't want to join the men in the kitchen, their voices bright as they jostle verbally with each other. Instead we open the tall doors as wide as they go and crowd on to the sill, feeling the night air cool our faces.

"Think how angry Mother would have been to see that," Grace says, and we all make quick guilty chirrups that are not really laughing. She would hate such a scene. She would have punished us without a second thought.

James comes into the dining room carrying a tray that has three china cups on it. He places it and we watch the steam rise up warily.

"Cocoa," he says. "Just powder and water, I'm afraid." He makes an apologetic gesture. Llew joins us. Neither of them mentions my sisters tormenting Gwil in the woods.

I am the first to drink from my cup, everyone watching me. It tastes good. They have used plenty of powder, and some of the grains have not dissolved. They stick behind my teeth, leaving a sweet film on my lips.

They coax us into the lounge. At first the men sit at the opposite side of the room, but soon they come over to where we huddle, all three of them. They plant their bodies too close to us. We can feel the heat spreading from them, warming our own skin.

"We've been talking, you know," James says. He shares a look with Llew, who nods. "You could come with us, when we're picked up. Wouldn't you like that?"

"No," says Grace. We move our heads in agreement with her.

"Don't throw the idea out yet," Llew said. "If your mother doesn't return—if she's left you for good—we'll protect you."

"She hasn't left us," says Grace.

"Of course, of course," says Llew. His voice is the voice of a person trying not to scare us.

"You have your whole lives ahead of you," adds James, and I look at him and hate the quivering set of his mouth, the peeling skin at his nose.

"They'll come for us," Llew explains. "And we could bring you along. We would hate to leave you here alone."

"We won't be alone. Please stop talking," says Grace, placing her hands over her ears. Llew takes them and moves them to her lap, and the three of us stiffen.

"Don't be so childish," he says. I hate that he has touched her, and move my shoulder closer to his body to get more contact.

"Just think about it," says James. "Think about it."

"We wouldn't survive," says Grace.

I try to meet Llew's eyes, to give him a signal that I want this, that I want to stand with him in a new world the way we have spoken of, but he is not looking at me. His eyes are fixed out of the window, where the sea is a breathing animal.

He stays in my room that night, the first time. We don't discuss it, but when the dark of the night has deepened, when I have been lying there for a while, the door opens. He comes in and he pushes me with both his hands from the centre of the bed, whispers, "Move up." He doesn't close his arms or legs around me, doesn't do any of the things we normally do, just curls up with his back to me, his body close and hot. Soon his breathing dulls. I put my hand out to the back of his head, take hold of a palmful of his hair. Skull fragile underneath. I could kill him here, if

I wanted. I put my lips to his shoulder, very gently, so that he will not feel it.

In the night I wake up briefly and his body is shaking. I drape my arm across his stomach, bury my face into his neck. Possibly he is crying. As soon as I touch him, the shaking stops. He doesn't say anything. He could be embarrassed, or my touch could have mended him. I prefer the second option. I prefer the idea that my body, as the object of love, has a power I could never have dreamed of.

It was no one big thing but many small things. Each one chipped away at me. By the end, I felt skinless. My cuticles bled. I was aged immeasurably. I felt terrible that I had so little in reserve, that the other women could cope. It felt like I had failed them.

ON THE FOURTH DAY without Mother, I wake to the empty bed. My first action is to pull the covers off, to inspect the sheets feverishly for proof Llew was there at all. There are dark hairs on the pillow, shorter than mine. I bury my face into it, but we are all using the same soaps, unlabelled, slabs of carbolic salmon-pink and fat in the palm. I look for salt hardened on the pillowcase to prove that he was crying, but my search is inconclusive. More hairs on the sheet, the faint scent of his sweat.

My stomach turns without warning. I strip the bed and pile the sheets in the middle of the floor. I run a bath so hot that sitting down in it is almost unbearable, but I do it anyway. I think of the phrase **pain threshold** like it's a vault you jump. I have forgotten to open the window and steam fills the room in no time.

Quickly, before I lose my nerve, I make two minor, conciliatory slices in my thigh, a centimetre each. It is hard sometimes to tell which marks on my legs are from the summer I grew four inches, and which are the marks that keep us safe. The historical unwieldiness of my body is everywhere. Now there are new shames and new dangers, like how I have made noises, lost control, begged Llew to do things to me in ways that make me glad of the water's pain. The vaporous bath pinkens around me.

I drink a lot of water, to protect myself against those things I am doing with him. One pint, two, swallowed along with air, too quickly, standing at the sink. My stomach swells underneath my dress. I imagine the water cleaning my blood and lie down for a second on the balding velvet couch in the lounge while it works on me, listening to the sound of my body recalibrating.

Without Mother no bread is being made, the goat isn't giving up her milk, we are too scattered to keep the house in order. Breakfast leaves everyone hungry. The tins are vanishing swiftly, and Llew insists we open four of them. Peach slices, prunes, fruit cocktail, condensed milk that we spoon directly into our mouths. He doesn't give me any sign that the night before even happened when he turns up with Gwil in tow. The sweet food is making him sick, he tells us. He takes the opener off me because I am working through the tins too slowly, his own hands twisting them open in seconds.

"My teeth are about to fall out," he says, opening up his mouth to demonstrate. Gwil copies him. Both sets of teeth are hard and wolfish as usual, whereas ours do blacken at the backs of our mouths, me and my sisters'. The wet, red holes of the men's throats make me nauseous.

"You should have more variety in your diets," he tells us strictly. "Women your age. You should have red meat. Calcium. Folic acid. Your bodies have needs."

My body does not feel good. The fruit is too sweet, he is right. It sits and curdles in my stomach. I am still finishing my meal when Llew stands up and leaves the table, his bowl and spoon lying there carelessly. He has left some juice. When everybody else has gone, I take the bowl and drink the juice myself, panicked, unable to help it.

. . .

I find my sisters in the swamp-smelling heat of Grace's room, lying on her floor with the windows closed, the silk scarves Mother gave to us covering their bodies. It makes me start to see them lying there like that, unmoving, when I push the door open. Grace sits up, the silk falling from her face. The circles around her eyes are deepening like a bruise with every day. She observes me, does not say a thing.

"Can I join you?" I have to ask. She lies back down.

"If you want," she says. "We're meditating on a word."

It's an old technique used by Mother to calm us. Sometimes she would pick a word we had never heard before. It was like a treat, a small thing made of sugar. "Think about that," she would tell us. "Until you're bored. Until you fall asleep."

"What's the word?" I ask. Grace sighs.

"Tramadol," she says, pronouncing it slowly. "From the medicine cabinet." Her breath is sweetly bad, milk on the turn.

I move the word's contours over and over in my mind, the sheer fabric moving out with my breath. Despite the smell of my unwashed sisters filling my nostrils, lying here is soothing. I think of the small white pills, small blue pills, the glass of water, the brown glass bottle. Our mouths open, heads heavy. Grace, after the week we spent asleep, learning to keep what she was given under her tongue, spitting it out after Mother had left and displaying it in her palm for us to see. **Look,** she would say. **This is inside the both of you now**.

Sky sits up first. She finds a pair of scissors in the drawer next to Grace's bed and brings them to us.

"Will you cut my hair?" she asks me. I snip off the ends where they straggle, a centimetre or two, but she shakes her head.

"All of it," she says.

I am horrified by the idea. I say no and she pleads. Without her hair, she could fall sick. King insisted that we grew it as protection. But she turns her attention instead to Grace, who says, "You can do what you want." She puts her arms around Sky. She is doing it to spite me.

"What about what King said?" I ask.

"What about him," Grace replies. "We had shorter hair once. You probably don't remember that," she addresses Sky. "But we did."

Together they go into the bathroom and close the door. I study the chewed-up ends of my fingers. **Snip-snip,** go the scissors, even through the wood. When they come out, Sky's dark hair is clipped short around her ears. I look at her with fear.

"That's better," she says. She gives a short twirl.

It makes her look a lot older, as if she has caught up with us in one leap. She turns and examines herself in the mirror of the dressing table. Grace admires her handiwork as I take one deep breath and then another.

"You look pretty," Grace says. "The men will get ideas. Don't let them take liberties."

"Don't be disgusting," says Sky. She mimes retching.

"It is disgusting," agrees Grace. "I'm glad you think so." They don't look at me. My face is hot, flaming with blood.

We let her gather her own hair, sorting it into small piles, for her to do what she wants with. Offerings. Protections. Perhaps she will plant some in the garden and a new tree will push soft claws through the ground. I watch her closely for signs of sickness. Maybe I am already too late to save my own body, but I will do what I can for my sisters, despite their ingratitude. When she has finished, I am the one who walks her to Mother's bathroom and removes the aspirin from the medicine cabinet. She opens her mouth, closes her eyes, and I put one tablet on her tongue, two, and then I put one in my own mouth too, because even though I no longer feel nauseous there is a sense of dread starting to build at the edges of my body. Something that feels like it could be a symptom, something that really started days ago when Llew was on top of me and I opened my eyes to see his own fixed grimly on the wall behind the bed, as though I were incidental, as though I could be anybody.

James finds me crying in the garden, where I thought nobody would look. Somehow I am a child again and nobody wants to go near me, nobody can cope with how badly I want to be held, or touched, or listened to, and there is nothing I can ever do about it. I crouch my body down beside one of the ruined walls and sit in the grass, still wet with dew that soaks the skirt of my dress. There is a hot ball of anger at the centre of my pain. I find a sharp rock and put it in the palm of my hand, clutch it tightly.

"What's wrong with you?" I hear, and freeze. James sits himself next to me, not minding the sopping wet. He places out a hand to my arm but I flinch and he withdraws it.

"I hope we didn't upset you girls last night," he says. He is always calling us **you girls,** but I am just a girl now, my own girl, outside. Anything could happen to me.

"I'm not upset," I say.

"You can talk to me, Lia," he says. "What's wrong?"

I just cry harder. He sits and waits, and eventually, despite myself, I manage to say, "My sisters."

"What about them? Have you fallen out?" he asks, very gently. I wipe my eyes.

"Oh, Lia," he says. "I'm sorry to hear that." He pauses. "But you're old enough to be your own person. It's not healthy to be so dependent on your sisters, at your age."

I am ashamed.

"I used to hate my brother," he says, thoughtfully. "I wanted to kill him sometimes." I am silent suddenly, thirsty for knowledge, for anything about Llew. "And then he got sick. Very sick. We were still children. I thought he was going to die."

I try to think about Llew ill, small and vulnerable, but I cannot imagine him as a child. Instead my mind recalls the fluctuations in Grace's body through the years, always less hardy than mine. Two fevers, one severe enough for fasting diets, for salt in a line at the door frame of her room. A ballooning ankle, wasp-stung, the poison far from the heart. None of it preparation for the final change in her body.

"It made me realize what being brothers meant," James continues, watching me. "I never lost that, even when he recovered. You can't disregard blood, can you?" He pauses. "So this will pass, whatever it is. I know it."

You don't know anything, I want to tell him. My blood is disregardable, despite what he thinks, and yet everything I am belongs to them, if they want it. I want to laugh. I want to gesture at the world around me, the house, the forest, the garden falling away behind us. **There are no parallels,** I want to tell him. **Some things will never pass**.

He gives me a small and satisfied smile, gets

to his feet, brushes the grass and dirt from his trousers. “Why don’t you come with me, back inside? You’ll get too hot out here.”

“Mother,” I say. “I have to watch for Mother.”

He sighs again, but nods. “If you insist.”

Sky has a nightmare. Dozing on the terrace in the long afternoon light, we watch her arms jerk and twitch. Her mouth open in an **O** of pain, her newly shorn hair. I do not say **I told you so** to Grace, despite the temptation. My sister lies with her knees bent, sunglasses on, rubbing Mother’s forbidden oil thoughtfully on to her legs and arms.

“I’m afraid,” Sky tells us when she wakes, sweating and alert, to see us staring at her. “But I don’t know of what.” There is a long silence.

“I think you should do a therapy,” Grace says. “It’s been a long time.”

Sky shakes her head.

“I think it will help,” Grace continues. She looks at me. “Lia?”

I do not want to hurt my sister again. I feel the sweat gathering at my sides, under my dress.

"Please," Sky says. "I don't want to." She twists the fabric of her towel between her hands and screams, a sharp, child's noise, a too-young noise, until we move to put our hands over her mouth. Grace holds the back of her hand against her forehead. Sky rolls dramatically on to the ground, looks up at us from there to gauge our reaction.

"I'm sorry," Grace says. "I think it's the best option." She moves to her knees and holds both Sky's trembling hands in her own.

When we were younger, Mother encouraged me to have a favourite toy, a thing carved by King from driftwood. One day she gave it to Grace while I was watching and said, "This belongs to her now." Later there was a period when they would give me more at mealtimes, systematically, keeping it up for days. Grace watched my plate, unblinking, and I defended it from her with my body.

We reacted each time, slapping each other hard around the face or pulling out whole locks of hair or gripping each other tight until our nails burst small red moons against the skin. Those parental interventions, strange experiments with our hearts, stopped at some point, like a childhood game might have, not long before Sky came along. I don't know who stopped them, but I know that sometimes when I wheeled around mid-fury, locked together with my despised and beloved sister, I caught King and Mother looking at us like we were unrecognizable, like we were no longer their children. It hurt us very much to see that look but we soon forgot about it, absorbed again in how it felt to hate and love and hurt each other, the new things, the old things.

We gather glass after glass from the kitchen, making several trips, and lay them out on the floor of Mother's bathroom. Passing through her empty bedroom, it still feels like she is just downstairs; there is only the hint of staleness in the air if you breathe closely. The last photograph of our family is still on the mantelpiece, an accusation, missing King like a portent, although he has never been in the photographs; he was always the photographer. When I open her bottom drawer, looking for a bolt of muslin we can use if needed, I find the other group portraits. Mother's hair expands, falls past her waist, recedes to her ears. My sisters and I grow tall suddenly, like trees. In my favourite, Grace is sitting on Mother's lap. She is staring right into the camera on its tripod. I cover the photos in Mother's underwear, the lace with the holes in and shimmering, flesh-coloured elastic. I would like to crawl under her bed and stay there for a minute or two, in the dark and the dirt, but there is no room for me.

One row of glasses contains salt water, the other row fresh water, as cold as the tap will run. Grace counts out the measures. We step around them, careful not to spill anything. Sky sits keening next to the toilet, her knees up to her chest. Grace massages her temples with the tips of her fingers.

"Give me strength," she says. "Stop acting like such a baby."

I hand Sky the first glass, salt water, and she makes a face as she sips at it, before unexpectedly swallowing the whole lot. She squeezes her eyes shut. Grace hands her another and she does the same, before turning to the toilet and throwing up. Her hands grip the toilet seat. One of the empty glasses is knocked over by her foot.

"Enough," I tell Grace, who is holding another glass of salt water.

When Sky stops, turning back to us weakly,

I hand her a tumbler of the good water. She drinks this with no problem, then a second and third in quick succession, waves away a fourth. We are kinder to her than Mother or King would be, and do not force her to drink it. Instead we clear space on the floor, balancing tumblers on the cistern, the counter, the edge of the bath, the windowsill. She stretches out her body, her face wet. We have done our duty. I walk out and leave my sisters sitting there, the light refracting over and over through the liquid and the glass.

In my own bathroom, later, I inspect all the new bruises that have bloomed on my skin since the men came. I hadn't noticed them happening at the time, but here they are. Perhaps there is a virus ripening inside my blood. Cells bursting with their own fruitfulness. Love as a protest within my body. Or perhaps it's just that I am unused to touch, am out of practice. Bodies do not lie. This all acts as proof that he has touched me here, here, here. I pinch the back of my forearm, an unmarked spot, with satisfaction.

I am still there when Llew comes in, without knocking, and catches me looking at myself, at the faint shadows on my arms, my legs, at the patch of gauze halfway up my thigh.

"Sometimes you terrify me," he says. But he is smiling, so it is fine.

If Mother returns, it will mean the end of love. It will mean no more of the long line of him against the sheets, a faded blue towel across his body. He has just showered. There is a small group of moles by his knee that I press my thumb to, a tangle at the nape of his neck in the damp hair.

Limit your exposure to the men, or find the one who doesn't wish you harm. I overheard that once, passed from one damaged woman to another, an urgent, murmured conversation I was not supposed to witness. **It's the men who don't even know themselves that wish you harm—those are the most dangerous ones. They will have you cower in the name of love, and feel sentimental about it. They're the ones who hate women the most.**

We have been so careful. We have been so good. But this time, when he slips out of the door as usual, he pauses for a second. "Hello, Grace," he says.

"Hello," I hear her say, voice sour.

"How's it going?" he asks. I shut the door quickly, stay close to it.

"Fine," she replies. "Just fine."

I hear his footsteps disappear and think we may have got away with it, but soon there is a knock. I do not let my body move. Grace tells me, "I know you're in there, I know it, I know it," her voice the hiss of air escaping a balloon, but I refuse to respond.

"I heard you," she says. "I wasn't fucking born yesterday."

No, I mouth to the white-painted wood, knotted like a muscle. **Please.** My eyes fill with shameful water.

"Do you know what you're doing?" my sister asks me as I wait there. She tells me my body is now in grave danger. "And your thoughts," she says. "Don't they feel jumbled? Don't they feel diseased?"

Yes, they do, but then **what's new,** I long to hiss back. Will you deny me even this happiness? But I don't need to ask to know that she would.

A change of tack. Her voice becomes mournful. She points out that I could be bringing something terrible upon us.

"Have you noticed signs? You might be contagious."

I worry a loose tooth in the bottom of my jaw with my tongue.

"Let me in," she asks. "I can take your temperature." It is a trick.

"Go away," I whisper. I sit on the carpet with my back to the door and look towards the bed, the sheets a mess. They might even still be warm. I want to wrap them around myself until I suffocate.

In the end she goes, but not before slamming her fist into the door and then crying at the pain in her hand, which is also my fault, and telling me that she's disappointed in me, that there's a real chance I am failing them.

"You're a selfish bitch," she says finally. Her footsteps move down the corridor, unhurried. We do not use that word on each other. I would rather she had hit me, got me right in the bottom of the stomach, much rather that than this word.

I hawk up phlegm and spit in the bathroom, brush my teeth frantically, repent repent repent, but already I know there is no staying away from him, I am a helpless animal, I am dead even as I walk.

I run away from the house, down the beach, the entire length of it, and nobody is around to see me—maybe they are watching from the windows but I don't care, I cannot care. My feet are bare and throw the sand up with every step. Forcing myself to go faster, I threaten to turn over on my ankle but right myself and sprint harder as penance, harder. The pain grows in my chest but it is only my lungs, an honest pain, not the treacherous one in my heart. I wait for the exhilaration but it doesn't come.

Near the rock pools I finally let myself stop. When I catch my breath, I stand as close as I dare to the ocean and scream out across it, holding the shapeless call until my voice peters out. The sound does not come back to meet me. My hand goes to my throat and I feel the hum of arterial blood somewhere above the tenderness of my voicebox.

The things I have done come back to haunt me. Small pulses of shame behind my closed eyes.

"Hurt Grace, or Sky will have to." Again on the beach, tools and muslin and my sisters, obedient, waiting for me to do what I had to do. I would prefer a million times to be hurt over hurting them. Grace lay down obediently in the sand, pulling her hair over one shoulder.

Even then her resentment must have been building as I wadded up the muslin and held it against her mouth and nose, her eyes dark and flickering over the white cloth, a blame that was inescapable. **You know I have no choice,** I tried to transmit through my hands, through my thoughts. She showed no reaction at first, but by the end she was biting viciously through the cloth. I knew it was involuntary. I knew I would be doing the same.

Then, once Grace was recovering, it was time for me to hurt Sky. Maybe it was just a test of my loyalty, a test of how adequate was my love for my sisters, my love for her. Well, it was abundant, I would have told her if she had just asked. Love enough to make you sick.

For Sky, Mother made me rub a piece of sandpaper against the top of her arm, a place that wouldn't get infected. And I did it so that Grace wouldn't have to do it, so Grace could sleep that night and nights thereafter, Sky begging me not to even as her skin goose-pimpled with blood. "Please, Lia," she asked, closing her eyes. "I'll do anything." She let out a high noise from between her teeth, a constant pitch, like a stinging insect. It was unbearable. Afterwards she lay flat on the sand next to Grace as Mother bandaged her arm, holding it high above her so it would not be contaminated with sand or dirt. I went away and threw up into the sea, as usual. Light, light, light. The water washed it away at once.

The nights after hurting my sisters were always my worst. I made sure my physical suffering matched theirs, so I wouldn't be left behind. I stood next to the window without any lights on, my thighs stinging, gauging the sea's reaction. A dull harmony of pain, three notes reaching out across the water like a beacon. I could feel it reach the border, the signal finding purchase.

If we were to spit at them, they would spit back harder. We expected that—we were prepared for it even. What we didn't expect was their growing outrage that we even dared to have moisture in our mouths. Then outrage that we had mouths at all. They would have liked us all dead, I know that now.

ON THE FIFTH DAY without Mother, my body starts to fail me. When I wake up I am drowning, but it is not water covering my face. Nosebleed. My pillow is spattered with red. It slides into my mouth. I pinch the fleshy part of my nose as I hold myself up above the sink in my bathroom. When I grit my teeth, they are covered in it too.

My nightgown is ruined. I step into my bathtub still wearing it, spray myself with hot water before pulling it off, letting the fabric cuff around my ankles. The bleeding stops. I say a frantic prayer for my own health to the water, something about **please** and **sickness** and **don't let my sisters know.** I wring the nightgown out and wrap it in a brown paper bag, then another, then put it in a drawer.

What will happen if I have to crawl into the forest, my body a thing stricken, a thing radiating disease? Will my sisters stand over me among the foliage, or will they just watch me go, their bodies silent and upright on the terrace?

The women who stopped coming to us, they had known love too. They were in retreat from that, and from the world. We watched their personal acts of repair, both physical and spiritual. It was beautiful to see, Mother pointed out. A woman becoming whole again. It's true that, after the water cure, their bodies had a new solidity, as if somebody had redrawn their outlines. Their eyes were clear, ready to return.

That they have stopped coming could mean the world has improved, or that it is worse than ever. That they are dying on distant shores in their dozens, hundreds, thousands. That they are living lives of violence, their bodies shaped by it, their words painful, the air a jagged mess in their throats. I hope it is the first answer. I wish for them a cool equilibrium, lives of harmony. Muslin cocooning their faces, powerful talismans to ward off danger. Men who will be good to them. Whose bodies are not too fearful.

. . .

Llew is morose by the pool. He drinks from a brown glass bottle, raising it to me when I approach his recliner. "Found them in the cellar," he tells me. "Try it." I take a sip, warm and fizzing in my mouth. I spit it on to the floor automatically, comically, but he does not find it funny. "Don't be disgusting, Lia," he says. "What a waste." His tone is dark.

I lie silently on the recliner next to him for a while. My body feels anchored to his, pointless without his presence. Eventually he rises and heads inside, and I follow his lead. He sighs. "Are you my shadow now?"

I would like that, actually, but I don't tell him so.

His mood lifts slightly when we are out of the blazing sun, when we are looking at each other in the kitchen among the steel and tiles. He has something he wants to show me, in his room. Something that will cheer me up. "Because you're not yourself either," he tells me, "I can tell," and it is good to be seen but also terrible. I wait outside his room in the corridor, picking at my nails. He calls me in.

"Ta-da," he announces, spinning in a circle. He is wearing King's white linen suit, the same one, stiff lemony blooms under the arms. In the light from the window I can see his eyes are red. It is a little too long in the arms but otherwise fits perfectly. Even the buttons do up. I step back.

"You don't think this is funny?" Llew asks me. "Come on." He looks down at himself. "Look at me! It must have belonged to a guest. A real character."

The suit flatters him. I can picture him standing with his feet firmly planted on the wood of the terrace, a softer time. Looking out to sea, waiting for something, analysing the signs of the waves. Oh, this man that I love.

"It is funny," I say eventually.

If not the protective suit, with its years of weathering, then what could Mother have worn? Her whole body wrapped in muslin so she would be padded should she fall, bolts of it stuffed into her mouth? I don't want to think about it.

We go together to my room without discussing it, the routine of the past days, but when I lift up my dress he barely sees me, instead falling heavy on to the bed, the suit now forgotten. He becomes difficult again.

"I don't know if I want to," he tells me.

"Why not?" I ask.

"I just don't feel like it," he says.

"Please," I say, angry all at once, scared somewhere underneath it.

"Oh, Lia," he says, misinterpreting me, reaching out to cup my chin in his palm. "Don't. I didn't mean to upset you."

It works, anyway. He hesitates at times, as if wondering whether he is going too far.

"Keep going," I say to him during those pauses—once, twice, three times—and so he does, his hand tight around my throat.

Afterwards, I feel dizzy. My body is tied in a knot, heart pushed up to my throat. When I kneel at the toilet, nothing comes up. He sits on the edge of the bathtub, watching me retch.

"Don't go getting pregnant on me," he says. He sounds nervous.

"What?" I ask.

"What do you mean, **what**?" he says.

"Nothing," I say, standing up slowly.

"You're taking precautions, aren't you?" he asks.

I think of the water gulped in pints, the

wounds on my legs, the hot water, the showers. "Yes," I say, overcome with tenderness suddenly at this proof of his care for me.

"All right," he says. "Well, we probably should have discussed this earlier. But if you're being careful." He scratches at the back of his neck.

My vision strobes, a split second of darkness. I am still dizzy, still confused, unwilling to put the pieces together.

"I'm going to lie down," I tell him. I hope he will stay with me, but he turns off the light and closes the door as he leaves, no kiss, just one small gesture of the hand.

I remember Mother keening on the floor of the kitchen, King still alive then. Her arms were around her knees; her body was in the foetal position. The moonlight made her hair look like water, spilling out from its ties. And me, mute, standing there thinking, **Use a blanket, use anything, why are you lying down there when there is a warm bed somewhere above you, when there are people with their arms open for you?** Anger too, because she was loved. **Mother, there is really no need.** But now I can understand why you would lie down there, why you would seek out a place that is hard and cold.

It's James, not Llew, who hovers above me when I wake. I have slept until dinnertime. "I was sent to get you. Come on," he says. The air is thick with my sleep, curtains closed. I see him take in the disorder, the things strewn around.

"Where's Llew?" I ask, single-minded.

"Downstairs, doing something or other," he says. "He said you were feeling poorly earlier. Are you still dizzy?"

I look into his concerned face and nod.

"Keep hold of me for a second, then," he says. I grasp his arm as I rise up. "Ah. You need to put some clothes on though," he adds, averting his eyes, and I realize I am just in my underwear, that I pulled off my clothes somewhere in the dead expanse of the afternoon. I don't care particularly about him seeing me like this. The damage has long been done. He locates my dress on the floor, a puddle of linen.

"Turn around and put your arms up," he tells me. "I won't look."

The cool fabric passes over my head, down

my body. I wonder for a second if I want him to touch me, or if it's just that I want to be touched by anyone. When he entered the room, for a few seconds in the gloaming light he could have been Llew. I am used to compromises.

"That's better," he says, doing it up at the neck. "You're decent now. Fit for company." He gives me a kind pat on the shoulder.

"When will Mother be back?" Sky asks Grace at dinner, fretfully. I push cold tinned peas around my plate and use the back of my fork to crush them, slowly, into a paste.

"Tomorrow," says Grace, after a pause.

"Do you promise?" Sky asks.

I wait for Grace to say yes, but instead she stands up. She is still holding her cutlery. Looking at it with something approaching wonder, as if she has no idea where it came from, she throws it down to the floor. It clatters on the parquet. She walks out. We watch her go. James springs up to follow her.

"Leave her," I warn him. I move to pick up the fork and knife myself, crawling on the ground under four silent gazes. Sky stands and follows our sister. I stay.

The men talk vigorously to each other. They have all gained colour in their cheeks, on their arms. Gwil seems like a different child, no longer lank and wistful. He taps out a tune with his knife on the edge of his plate, and neither Llew nor James tells him to stop it, engaged in their conversation about someone they know from elsewhere, some other man. I don't care about any other man. Gwil stares at me, daring me to make him stop, then taps louder. I want to throttle his small throat, but I don't.

After dinner I open door after door, searching for my sisters. They are not in the lounge, not in their bedrooms, not in Mother's room. Eventually I find Sky alone in one of the unused rooms a few doors down from mine, stretching in the light by the window. Her short hair is still a shock to me. She doesn't seem like one of us any more, but then maybe I am the one who has changed irrevocably, has taken in the new love. Maybe we were never three branches of the same tree, three girls intertwined.

"Where is Grace?" I ask. Sky gestures at the closed en-suite door.

"She's taking a bath," she tells me. "Go on in, if you like."

I knock at the door and Grace's low voice tells me to enter. She is almost totally submerged, a fine froth of bubbles covering her entire body, beading her dark hair. It is cut short like Sky's now, I can see as she moves up in the water, exposing her whole head. The curtains are closed. When I sit on the edge of the bath and dip my hand in the water, it is cold. Her toenails, breaking the surface, are painted cerise, like Mother's were.

"Sky painted them for me," Grace says when she sees me looking. "She'll probably do yours, if you ask." She moves back under the water, sending it splashing up the side.

"Your hair," I say uselessly, conscious of my own lying heavy down my back. Grace puts a hand to her head.

"Yes," she says. "Sky was right. It's a lot more comfortable like this." She points to the metal wastepaper bin in the corner. "It's all in there. You can look at it if you want."

I do not want.

"The water's cold," I tell her instead.

"I prefer it that way," she says. "It's too hot anyway." She fixes her eyes on me. "Have you noticed how much warmer the men have made it?"

"It's coincidence," I say weakly, not even believing myself. Water runs off my skin in the night like something doused. Mosquito bites rise behind my knees and ankles. I am weary, so weary, of moving this body around through the haze.

"Bullshit," she says cheerfully. "It doesn't matter, anyway. Not now. Let the whole world melt, for all the difference it will make. Let the whole thing fall apart." A little water trickles over the lip of the bath, pools on the tiles. She sinks her head under the milky surface and I watch anxiously until she rises up again with a deep breath, hair slicked against her scalp.

"We're not doing anything wrong," I tell her.

"You've betrayed us," she says simply.

"It's not true," I say. I know that it is.

"Lia," she says. "He is dangerous." She buries her head unexpectedly into her wet hands for a second but does not cry.

"Don't think you're the only one suffering," Grace says, raising her face back to mine. She is so beautiful. Whatever she is feeling, it is not written upon her the way it is upon me. And I think, for a second, about the first time my father placed a sharp object in my hand. How using it made a deep and terrible sense, because my blood was even redder than my sisters' blood. It ran thicker. My feelings were as physical, as measurable, as the pulse at my neck.

"I've decided to forgive you, though," she says after a long pause. "I know you need my help."

I cry at that. **I do, I do.**

"First things first," she says. "Protect your body from now on."

How, I ask, salt water running into my mouth.

She tells me I can add vinegar to my bath, bicarbonate of soda. I should salt the water at the very least, have it as hot as possible, hotter than is pleasant.

"No more babies," she says. "They never came from the sea, of course."

I stare at her. I realize what Llew was telling me earlier. I realize, finally, what she really means.

"Do not ask me about that," she says, reading my thoughts. "Not ever."

So I don't. My hair, I ask instead, falling out where I pull at it. And my ears, and my eyes, and my heart.

"Just don't look too closely," she says. "Try to have less direct contact. Touch him through his clothes, if you must."

I am stricken.

"If you can't, you can't," she says, resigned. "You're the one who will suffer most."

Truce.

Shifting in the water, Grace seems to take me in as if for the first time, as if I had just walked in. She stares at my legs, and I pull the skirt of my dress down.

"I often think that Mother and King were very cruel to you." She touches my hand with her own. "I wish things could have been different."

Perhaps it is not too late. I ask her if we can go to Mother's room, the three of us, and she appraises me from the water, drawing her knees up to her chest.

"All right," she says, reaching a hand out to me. "Help me up."

The skin of her fingertips is pruned and furrowed against my own. I hold out the towel for her to step into, notice the fragile ridge of her hipbones under her still-swollen stomach. We are weakening.

In Mother's room we stand in front of the irons. The blank iron, shining and shameful.

"Why don't we pick again?" I ask my sisters. "With Mother not here. Why don't we just get the men to join us, pick with them?" I look around at them, gauging support for the idea. "Or even just the three of us pick?"

They remain quiet. It's natural to avoid the broken thing, to distance yourself from it.

"I really don't think it will solve anything, Lia," Grace says finally. My chest aches. I cough to try to relieve it.

"Well, that's that, then," I say, and we leave the room as quickly as we entered. Grace puts her arm around Sky's shoulders so easily, her wet skin leaving the back of her dress transparent. The soaked fabric is thin and blue, and for a second I think of a ghost, the loose pucker of limbs. I have to shake my head to get the image out.

I decided I would take matters into my own hands, that I too could be vengeful. I would make him dissolve with fear like an aspirin in the glass, I would have him fall to the ground and beg me for mercy. Why not? There was only me, my women wanted no part of the plan. They told me I would die trying. I told them I didn't care. And I didn't.

ON THE SIXTH DAY without Mother I go straight outside after waking, not bothering to eat. There's no one around as I move through the corridors, and for a second I permit myself the fantasy that a boat has come, that everyone else has been taken up on it. But it's only enjoyable because it's not real. If the last year has taught me anything, it is that being alone is corrosive. I am a person unable to handle it.

I collect a long fingertip of dust from the lip of a vase, a solitary object on the mantelpiece in the hall. It is empty except for a wasp dying in its own sound, vibrating dully against the porcelain. **Suffer,** I mouth at it.

Somewhere in the night, alone in the bed once more, I woke up and realized there is nothing I wouldn't do for him. It felt very simple with no other thoughts, without the detritus of everyday sensations, preoccupations. A reminder of how straightforward love can be, sometimes, when it all falls into place.

. . .

I find Llew playing tennis with Gwil, and I sit cross-legged on the sandy dirt outside the court, picking at my nails, listening to the sound of them batting the ball back and forth. Gwil's shouts of "Yes!," Llew's answering laugh. He must be letting the boy win. Dust stipples my feet in my sandals. I dig my nails into my shin, near to my ankle, so it looks like an insect or a snake could have bitten me. It seems like for ever before the two of them come out of the court, both sweating. Llew gives Gwil a slap on the hand, arms raised high, and turns to me.

"What's up?" he asks, the smile on his face falling a little. Gwil swats his racquet around, listening to us.

"I just thought I'd come and find you," I say, self-conscious. "To see if you wanted to do something." I do not say **anything, we can do anything you want,** not in front of the child, though if he was not there I might fall to my knees on the ground and beg.

"I'm busy," he says. "Sorry." He turns to Gwil. "Another game?" The child nods. As they walk back on to the court, I run behind them. When I grab hold of Llew's arm, he stops.

"Please," I say, my mouth dry. "Please. You don't understand." He tries to draw his arm away, but I cling on. He pushes me once, then again, more forcefully, but I do not let go.

"Don't move!" I tell him, too loudly. "Please." I can feel love slipping past me like a fast breeze. Like draining water. I am ready to humiliate myself, if that is what it takes. He pushes me a third time and I fall back, stagger hard to the ground. I am on my knees after all. Gwil looks at me in alarm.

"What's wrong with you?" Llew asks me, rubbing at his arm.

"Nothing!" I say. "But stay with me. Stay." I get up, lunge for him again, but he just steps back further.

"Can you not, in front of the boy?" Llew demands. "Can you please be normal for a second?"

I do not know why loving like everyone else is so unnatural to me. Llew holds up his hands, beckons for Gwil to shelter behind him, as if I am dangerous, as if I am repulsive. Maybe I am. **He must know,** I think, as if in a trance. **He must be able to tell what is going on, even at his age. He's still a man. This is still all his to come, his heritage, his right.**

"This is all getting a bit much, isn't it?" says Llew, attempting to be kinder, to defuse the situation. "What has got into you?" A small pause. I understand that he is trying to shame me for my need, but unfortunately for him and for me I am totally shameless in this regard, I will demonstrate my need over and over for anyone who asks. I would take my strange and incapable heart out of my chest if I could, display it, absolve myself of responsibility.

When I slap him, hard, in the face, his first reaction is surprise.

"You just hit me," he says, feeling out the damage, which is minimal. "Didn't think you had it in you."

Gwil drops the racquet. He runs to the other end of the court, bleats for someone to come and help, but nobody is around.

I try to lash out at Llew again but he grasps my wrists, holds them tight to immobilize me.

"Right," he says. "I've had just about

enough of all this." He shakes me. "Pull yourself together."

The mark my body has left on his is fading already. My whole strength has barely any effect. My anger cannot touch him, cannot even be taken seriously. He is moving away from me all the time.

"We had a good thing going on, I know. But I don't fucking **belong** to you," he tells me as I give up the struggle and stand there before him, cowed, staring at him with stinging eyes. He still holds both of my wrists painfully, my palms grazed. I cannot move and I do not want to. "I don't think I've done anything to give you that impression."

It occurs to me that I have never heard him say the word **love** out loud. This could be the moment when he will say it. He releases his grip on me and his hand comes towards my face; I feel his knuckles stroke my cheek, gently. The moment passes.

They leave me on the court. I throw mouldering tennis balls against the ground until my arm aches; I kick the mesh until I am bored of my own melodrama. The sky darkens with rain. When I go inside I come across James alone in the lounge, sitting on the sofa. I flick the light on, then back off. I watch him from where I stand.

"Drink?" he asks, holding up a bottle. "Bit early, I know."

"That stuff will kill you," I say.

"Everything will kill you," he tells me, taking a sip from his glass, which is crowded with ice. He has everything he needs to keep him comfortable, but it seems to be doing him no good. "When you get to my age, you'll stop caring about your body."

"You're not that old," I say. He's not, it's true, I recognize with surprise. Hair covers both their chins now, and while James's is greyer than Llew's, it's not a huge difference.

"Too old for all of this," he says into his glass. He looks directly at me. "Are you happy? I'm interested to know."

Something surges up in my throat, and he sees it. "I didn't mean to upset you," he says. "Here. Sit down." He pats the cushion next to him and I sit on the edge.

"You poor girls," he says, almost to himself. "Alone here for so long." He puts his hand on my back, delicately. An idea comes to me. "Well. We can protect you now, can't we?"

I shuffle my body closer to his, lean my head on his shoulder. He is warm and smells of brine. He has been kind and good to me. When I kiss him, it's not dreadful at all. He returns it. He puts his hands on my face, my neck, my shoulder, but then he stops, he shakes his head and stands up.

"I'm sorry," he says. "I shouldn't have done that."

"Don't you want to?" I ask. "Was it bad?" I grope for the rough knuckles of his hand. He looks stricken.

"Lia," he says, taking his hand away. He sits down heavily on a chair across the room. "Of course I want to. You're lovely." He stares at his knees. "It wouldn't be right. We're not here for that."

"But I want to," I say, made bold, made desperate.

"We have a duty of care," he says. "I'm sorry. I just can't."

I stare at the floor as James pinches the bridge of his nose and think of other ways I could hurt Llew.

A trap rigged up in the forest to break his ankle, his arm, his neck.

Lure him into the sea.

Broken glass in his food.

"I'm a sad case, Lia," James tells me. He laughs harshly. "It's terrible to be a man, sometimes."

I find it hard to believe him. It doesn't seem that terrible, all things considered.

The anger again, an anger I can't call new because it feels too familiar, it feels like something that has been waiting for me all along. The women's pain had to stick around somewhere. Captured by the topsoil, atmospheric remnants, calcifying into pebbles moved by the sea. We had eaten and breathed it, made it our own.

Years ago, King taught us about lifeguarding. Perhaps he had foreseen the men coming for us. Perhaps he knew more than he let on. I always thought of my beloved father as omniscient. Something had broken the world's mysteries open to him, as if what we saw and knew was only a carapace, and underneath lay the true and strange heart of the universe, otherwise inaccessible.

"It's hard for me to teach you this," he admitted as we stood in the ballroom with three small knives at our feet. Gifts from him. "I thought about getting your mother to do it. But in the end, I decided it wasn't appropriate."

Mother wasn't there. She was taking a stretched-out afternoon bath, somewhere above our heads, oil floating on the water. A mask of milk and salt on her skin, to soften it. She already knew all about this.

"There may be a time when the border no longer works, when the toxic air moves across the sea," he said. "There may be a time when you find yourselves bleeding from the mouth, or eyes. There may be a time when we are no longer here to protect you."

We picked up the knives and copied his motions. Graceful. I imagined the air cleaving, my skin parting. King held the blade to his own neck, a few centimetres away.

"Like this," he said, and we did as he did, drawing our knives in a line once, twice, three times. "Easy enough."

"Easy," Grace agreed. His eyes flicked to her. She moved the knife one more time, then placed it carefully on the floor.

. . .

This is what I do. I leave James hunched in his chair and go to Mother's room. I take every iron down, placing them in the cloth bag from which they are drawn every year. The air is cooling as I walk with the irons through the garden, through sweet mulch and pooling water, the rotting things. On the way I look at the dead mouse behind the wall, its rib cage now exposed to the elements, its skull too. **Help me.** The forest looms. It is dark in here, dark where I belong, with the wolves and the snakes and the other loveless creatures.

In a tree trunk that has fallen and been hollowed out with decay, I hide the irons, and I am crying now, oh, I have gone and done it. Mother will be so angry at me when she returns. She may send me away. But this is what a lack of love does to a person, I will tell her, I can explain. This is what happens when you can no longer bear it. I will tell her that all of this has been an awakening, this fever dream, this discovery. My blood glowing with the new disease. There is not much time left for me, I feel, but still I will tell her, when she returns, holding her hands with a deep compassion, that I have meant this as a reparation. I have meant this as my most sincere act of love.

I make dinner wearing latex gloves that snap satisfyingly on to my hands. A new skin, better than the old. I am tenderly conscious of not bringing my sisters down with me, of protecting them better than I have done myself. The meal is what I can manage from the tins, the dried foods, a few crabs that James caught and smashed open. But nobody eats much. Llew does not turn up, and after our incident on the court I still shake to think of him. The cicadas drone so loudly that we close the windows, forcing them into their warping frames. My sisters chew and spit, chew and spit, complain. The skin of their elbows and knees is chapped, like mine, from sun and salt water. I keep the gloves on while I eat and nobody comments. Washing up, my hand becomes a dead claw in its soaped balloon of plastic; I fight the compulsion to hack it off with the meat cleaver.

After dinner, the three of us are together on the terrace when the sea reveals a new ghost. Sky sees it first and she screams. She has been screaming so much since the arrival of the men that we don't rush to her at once. But when she calls out "Ghost!" we sit up on our recliners, hurry to the railing. I reach for the binoculars she has dropped, and inspect them. Grace holds Sky but she pulls away, runs to the other end of the terrace and leans over, retching.

It is up to me to look. This ghost is closer, more recognizably human than the last one. Its skin is a washed-out blue, paler even than the baby, limbs inflated. Grace pulls at the binoculars and puts her mouth to my ear.

"Is it Mother?" she asks me. "Is it?"

"I can't tell," I tell her. Plausible deniability. "I can't tell." I pass her the binoculars and join Sky at the rail, heaving involuntarily all the way to the stony earth below.

Grace looks at the ghost for a long time.

"I don't think it is her," she says. "She would come to us."

"Is it moving closer?" Sky calls out. She is very pale.

"Possibly," says Grace. "I keep losing sight of it. We'll monitor it."

. . .

King once told us you can get used to anything, and it is strange how quickly the ghost becomes normal. Grace and I split the monitoring duties, so that Sky does not have to look at it again.

"Where do you think it came from?" I ask. She passes me the binoculars and I train them carefully on the air above the ghost, then the water, inching down until it fills my vision.

"The sea," she says. "It's giving up its dead."

"Why?" I ask.

"Because everything's becoming ruined," she says. Her eyes do not move sideways to look at me, but I know what she means.

The ghost isn't wearing a gown we recognize as Mother's. It doesn't seem to be wearing anything at all. It is too far away to make out the features and, honestly, I am glad. If it is Mother, I would rather not know.

As I watch the ghost move up and down in the surf, but not closer to shore, a fist of grief opens in my chest. There is a new wrongness in the air between us that threatens to engulf everything. This is what happens when the people you love leave you. This is what happens when the protection no longer holds.

I have been repenting for so long, but I

can't bear the burden of this guilt much longer. Leaving Grace out on the terrace, I sit just inside the corridor, on the faded carpet. This is the wrong place for me, this endless cramped tunnel with shadows heavy at either end, and the pressing silence without Mother is terrible, I can't ignore it any more. I retreat to one of the unused bedrooms and wait to catch my breath, thin air in shallow gulps, moving through on my hands and knees to the bathroom, where I feel momentarily safer. A place where faceless women have unloaded their own hurt, fabric dragging around their knees as they threw up bile and water, as they cried until there was no noise left to make.

Mother. The long dresses ragged at the hem. The strands of her hair that gathered in drifts, that fell on to the tablecloth at every meal and lay there, curled in long figures of eight. She had absorbed what it meant to be an attractive, healthy woman and we witnessed her body failing her daily with the guilt of voyeurs.

She told us all the time that she would give her life to us. I didn't care, because I thought that was just what mothers said. **Am I supposed to do the same for you,** I thought with something approaching horror, **because I am not sure I can.**

I have always been afraid of her ability to pull the rug out from underneath us, her capacity for cruelty and kindness in the same sentence, same action. I can see it in Grace too. It must be a prerequisite for being a mother, something that growing another person inside you does, heart and heartlessness, as though simplistic empathy has been scooped out and replaced with something more fundamental, something more likely to guarantee survival.

James is the one who comes looking for me, again. He kneels his large body down to my level, to where I am huddled under the sink. There is panic in his eyes.

"You saw it, didn't you?" he says.

I nod.

"Come with me," he says. "We are all downstairs." He puts out his hands.

The men are grim-faced, even Gwil. The three of them sit opposite us at the far end of the lounge. "Where did it come from?" we ask again and again, assuming they will know more than us. Grace scrutinizes their faces with a deep suspicion.

"Is it Mother?" she asks them straight out, and the men shake their heads vehemently.

"It must have come from the land," Llew says. "Something must be happening."

Clues, clues. The sky falling in. Earth cracking. Llew and James exchange looks.

"We don't want you to see it," James says. "We have to stay here until we know everything is safe."

The two men leave periodically to check, to walk around. As it starts to get dark Llew brings us water and crackers, a jar of jam with spoons, a ring-pull tin of rice pudding, then leaves again. We eat it warily, our eyes fixed upon Gwil, who doesn't say a word. He looks up past us, at the wall behind. Grace wipes her mouth with the back of her hand.

"Do you want some of this?" she says, holding out the tin of pudding. He shakes his head and she withdraws it.

"Baby," Sky says very quietly. "Stupid. Why don't you go home?"

Grace pushes her. "Stop that."

Sky shrugs her off. “Why don’t you talk?” she asks him. “Why don’t you stand up for yourself?”

He closes his eyes, as if he were very old and gathering patience.

I wonder, looking at his small and defeated face, whether he lives with the daily knowledge of the harm he could grow up to do. Whether it is there like a piece of paper folded up small around a secret word that he cannot yet understand. I wonder if Llew has caused damage to women before, and if so whether Gwil has borne witness to it, learned from it already.

“Your mother,” I say to him, the way my sisters did in the forest. He shakes his head, but I am not trying to hurt him, I am not doing it maliciously. “Where is she?”

He shakes his head again, harder this time. “I don’t want to talk about her,” he says. Water comes to his eyes. I move closer to him, nausea building once more. Behind me, my sisters are watchful.

“Baby,” Sky says again. “It’s just a question.”

Llew loved her enough to create another person from her flesh. She loved him enough to go through what Grace did, the animal room full of blood. The proof of the love sits in front of me, more tears now in his eyes, running down his face, and I am angry, I am so jealous all of a sudden of what he means, yet another love I will never claim.

"Tell us about your mother, Gwil," I say again. "Tell us about your women."

We gather around him. We put our hands on him to try and comfort him, his shoulders, his arms; we push him back a little. He is surely too small to do us real harm: we are suddenly giddy with this realization. We are not monsters. We are not trying to pull him apart. We are just women who want to understand.

I should have been kinder to him. I realize now I should have loved Gwil to make Llew love me better. All the ways in which I have fallen short, all the ways I could have done better. My hands become more frantic. The child shrugs us off, hitting at us, hard enough to hurt.

"Leave me alone," he says sharply, high-pitched, and we fall back. "Go away." He stands up and goes to sit behind the sofa, his usual place. We can hear him crying and for a short while I am ashamed, but it's not long before the sound dies down.

Soon after he slips out of the room. We feel so bad that we let him pass without question, leaving him alone in an attempt to make it up to him, to prove that we are not creatures to be feared or hated. We play rock, paper, scissors to decide who gets the last crackers, then lie down very bored on the rug, along the sofa. Grace switches on a small lamp that gilds her orange.

I do not know how long we lie there for, but at some point we realize that it is dark and Gwil has not returned. We are too afraid to leave the room, so we wait for James to come back. He shrugs when he finds just us, deciding Gwil must have gone to find his father.

When Llew comes back the child is not with him. My sisters and I are falling in and out of sleep, digging our nails into our palms or kicking our heels against the chairs, the floor, because to be asleep is to be defenceless. James looks puzzled. In an instant, everything changes.

We search with the sweeping light of torches. We examine everything. The dying grass of the lawn is long under our feet, under our hands when we kneel to check beneath bushes, behind trees. Llew is silent except when he shouts his son's name. I know enough not to touch him or go near.

The beach is empty too, the rowing boat lonely against the jetty. The waves make small sucking sounds. The three of us exchange looks. We remember the other times we have searched.

"Fuck," Llew says after we have checked inside the coal hatch. He kicks a clod of earth next to it, wheels around to stare away from us, up into the sky. "Fuck!"

Maybe the earth has swallowed him. Maybe the earth has swallowed our mother. Maybe we are being picked off one at a time. Something has stolen into our home and eaten them alive. The absence of our mother and the absence of Gwil become the same darkness. I am very afraid. Llew is not crying but his face is hard, and there is something unfurling in him, in all of us, as we walk around the garden's perimeter. Llew barks "Gwil!" again and again. I do not have a handle on my grief, on my panic, I do not know which is mine and which is Llew's. Love has made me self-centred, it has made me rank with greediness, I cannot think straight. When I stumble over a hard knot of wood at the outskirts of the forest, it is my sisters who lift me up from the dry earth.

In the house we gather in the lounge again, covered in sweat and dust. My sisters and I go to leave, but Llew stands up and blocks the door.

"You stay here," he says. "For your own protection." He looks murderous.

Grace tries to push past him and he holds her by the arms, effortlessly.

"Stay here," he says, more insistently. His fingers dig into her skin. I feel it like it's my own.

"I want to go to my room," Grace says. "I'm tired."

"You can sleep here," he says. His eyes slide between our faces. "On the couches."

James leaves, then comes back shortly with a canteen of water, a bucket. He places them near the fireplace.

"Good night," the men say, and before we

know what is happening they leave, the click of the door as it is locked from the outside.

Grace hurls her body against it and lets out a low howl from the back of her throat.

"So this is how it begins," she says, but of course it has already begun. It began for us a long time ago.

We stay awake. We keep a vigil. For the first time in months, we talk about King. We talk about Mother. I remind us of the time King caught a small shark and we ate its thick flesh, but first he hung it up in the garden, from a tree, so that he could take a good photograph as its blood stained the grass underneath. I put my hands inside its mouth, up to the wrist.

Grace reminds us of a day our parents were both drunk, a winter's day, how they lit the fire and we opened packets and packets of foods, ate it in a picnic on the floor of the living room with our hands feral, King pouring whisky into small, patterned glasses.

"Remember the time we hid in the attic," Sky says, "we waited in that cupboard all day long," and then we are back there, curled in the dark like dead flowers, because we had wanted to know how long it would take our parents to mind our absence. It took them maybe half a day; we all had limbs fizzing with sleeping blood, with the lack of our movement, yet we were able to stay so still for so long.

Everybody knew and nobody helped. It was the secret that we were all choking on. Even my mother, my sisters, my aunts. They passed it around. They said, with their eyes, why should you escape it? What makes you better than us? Can't you see our hearts have been bleeding for years?

ON THE SEVENTH DAY without Mother, the men unlock our door at first light. They are apologetic. Llew rubs his hand against my back even though the others can see him do it, and it kills me, the promise of being acknowledged for the first time. Nobody comments. The men bring us more food, tinned fruit cocktail, tinned pears, but it's not quite enough. When we've eaten, we move to search again. I team up with Llew, my sisters with James. We return to the forest, all of us.

We can see clearly now, in the light and the heat haze. The remnants of where animals have scratched and slept, the sweeping lines of snakes that have passed through the dirt, which Llew pauses to examine. The vipers are poisonous. They will stop your heart. They will make your fingers ulcerate and drop off one by one. I can't take my eyes away from the back of Llew's neck, the exposed patch of vulnerable skin that has reddened from the time outside, yesterday. It is peeling, it looks painful.

It is James who finds Gwil, just past the border, when the sun is high in the sky. Llew and I hear the whistle blow, Llew's neck snapping up as though someone has broken it. He runs without looking back.

When I see them gathered around the child, when I see his body, it is not difficult to picture what happened. The abrasions on Gwil's legs suggest he staggered through the border in the dark, caught his skin on the barbs, but that wouldn't have been enough to kill him. His arms and hands, torso and cheeks, have circles of red and white like targets. He is swollen, lumpish as an old pillow.

Hornets. They are native to our forest, swarming close to the ground with a great dignity. We used to run inside when they circled the lawn, staying low until they gorged themselves on sweet fruit and died or left. I picture Gwil determined, thrashing his way through the undergrowth past the border. He must have knocked against the nest and found himself overcome, the disturbed insects rising in a cloud.

. . .

The men carry Gwil's distorted body through the trees, and they blunder, they almost fall often but they do not let us help, they make terrible noises when we make any move to touch him. We trail behind, placing our feet very precisely around stones and twigs. In the house they lay him out in Llew's room, pushing the sheets and covers back. We stay outside the open door, watching them. The grief swells them. It catches in their chests. I know we need to get away from them. Llew is holding Gwil's hand with both of his and holding on too tightly; I can tell even from a distance he is crushing his fingers together.

"You frightened him," Llew tells us. He rounds on us. "You made him do it. What did you say to him?"

"Nothing," says Grace, very calmly. "He must have just wanted to go home."

It is mainly the truth and yet it still makes me heartsick.

Llew marches us to Grace's room. He produces the spare bunch of keys that once lay behind the reception desk.

"In there," he says. No sooner have we

stepped in than he closes the door, locks it. Grace doesn't hurl herself against it this time.

We get into the bed, and with our arms around each other we cry. When we feel too dehydrated, I am the one who gets up, fills a dusty glass with water from the bathroom and passes it around. In between the periods of weeping we listen out for the men. Grace lays out her life-guarding knife on the bedside table. "Just in case," she tells us. But nobody comes for us, nobody unlocks the door. We cannot hear the noises of the men with the blankets over our heads. Without the blankets they are very quiet, quiet enough for us to ignore, to pretend it is a trick of the wind.

When Sky has fallen asleep, Grace turns to me. Her feet are freezing against my shins. "You're always warm," she tells me. "Even now." The insinuation of change. I want to tell her, **It's still me.** Soon the pillow between us is wet.

"We're going to die," she says in my ear.

"Don't say that," I tell her, but it hangs above us, it has a ring of certainty. We are silent for a while.

"The baby was a boy, wasn't it?" she says, not a question but a statement. I breathe in, breathe out. I don't need to tell her yes.

"Maybe men can't survive here," she says. "Maybe that's how we are truly protected." A note of hope in her voice. I close my eyes.

"Grace," I say. "Grace. Do you think Mother is dead?"

She doesn't answer immediately.

"No," she says. "I don't." She turns over to face me. "Not after everything she's done."

"Where do you think she is?" I ask.

"I think she's lost," Grace says. "I think passing the border weakened her. I think she's out on the sea. Hurt, maybe. But still coming for us."

Sky wakes up. "Mother," she weeps. "Mother."

Shush, we tell her, **shush**. We shift around so that she moves into the middle, between me and Grace. We stroke her hair.

"She is still coming back," Grace says. "She will be here tomorrow. She will sail back over the sea, and the men will leave. They will go, and we will never see them again."

We wrap our arms around her. Soon she falls back into exhausted sleep.

"What do we do now?" I ask Grace very quietly, once I feel Sky's breathing slow.

"We wait," Grace tells me. "For as long as it takes."

Sky stays in the bed as Grace and I take it in turns to listen at the door, to shove at it with the force of our bodies. I try to pick the lock with a hairpin and do not succeed. I open every window in the room, in the bathroom, to hear what we can. The air, the reminder that the world still exists, is a shock.

Around midday, we hear the men speaking and moving past our room. We freeze, we make no noise, but their footsteps pass without interruption. From the window we watch as they carry Gwil's body across the beach underneath us, wrapped in a sheet. The shape of him dips and rises. Both men look terrible, even from a distance. James almost trips, but Llew is steady, a shovel strapped to his back. They move out of sight.

"They're taking him to the forest," Grace says.

I have had dreams before of women lying underneath the dirt and leaves, but not for a long time. The speculation of my treacherous mind.

A long time afterwards, the noise stops and the men return the way they came, grim and streaked with dirt. They must have rubbed their grimy hands into their eyes, down their cheeks.

The end is coming. We feel it like electricity, like the start of a migraine. When I part the curtains I am amazed not to see the water full of limbs. It is just the sea, as usual. A little rougher, perhaps. In Grace's bathroom I hit my elbow into the tiled wall, watch an inky bruise come up in the mirror.

I say a prayer for Sky, with her small and pliable movements, the way she came into the world and fitted so easily around us. I say a prayer for her collection of rocks and small animal bones, for the spray of her laugh, for her tan lines, for the dead sheaves of her cut hair, wherever she left it.

I say a prayer for Mother, for her hoarse voice and hands which never stopped moving, for her scented oils and eyeliner and insomnia, the menthol lozenges she held in her mouth like a bad word.

I say a prayer for King, wherever he is now. A prayer for his sincerity, a prayer for the holes in his T-shirts and the strange food he served up on the nights when it was his turn to prepare dinner, combinations designed to make us grow strong and healthful, tomatoes smeared with honey and oil, too much oil, they swam in it.

I say a prayer for the damaged women, for their thinning hair and cracked lips and offerings, for their rare arms around me during group prayer, for their distended stomachs filled with water and their wet clothes clinging to their bodies and their pain, their incomprehensible pain, which is now mine too.

A prayer for the baby, which would have been one of us; a prayer for its life, the small space of it that never got to happen. The prayer for the baby is just **I am sorry, I am sorry, I am sorry.** I pinch the bridge of my nose. My eyes in the mirror are red.

And I say a prayer for Grace, for her cold body and cold hands and cold heart, for her success where I have always failed, for the dirt behind her ears, for her hair filling my hands when I plait it, for her brutal honesty, for the animal smell of her body, for her distance. I say a prayer while wondering how I could ever have thought that we were two parts of the same person, knowing I would do anything to go back, to be there with her again, our hands clasped tight, held under the water by our father, and the light ribboning around us. I could have died there with her face close to mine and her pursed mouth and it would have been all right, it would have been a small mercy, but our father always brought us back to the surface, lifted us up into the sunlight and hot air as we coughed the water from our mouths.

Sometime during the long, sweltering afternoon there is a knock on Grace's door, then the sound of it being unlocked. We all look at each other.

"Hello," says Llew when I answer it. He is grey-faced but calm, wearing a clean shirt of King's. He peers behind me, into the room.

"Come downstairs," he says. "We made food." It could be a trap, but our stomachs complain with hunger. We follow him.

"We buried Gwil in the forest," says James as we eat pancakes made with just flour and water. Our dry mouths sip at too-weak coffee. "We wanted to do it as soon as possible." His voice catches. "We wanted to do it alone."

My sisters and I say nothing. The men do not talk about why they locked us in the room; they do not say anything further about Gwil's death being our fault.

We file out after the meal, but Llew catches me by the arm just before I leave.

"Stay," he says. "Come for a walk with me."

It isn't a question. I look to my sisters, and they nod.

We walk along the shore, just where the water hits the sand. Llew kicks at the ground. His face is sharp. I check reflexively for the dorsal fins of sharks, for more ghosts, but the sea is clear.

"How are you?" I ask. He laughs.

"How do you think?" he replies. "Not good, Lia. Not good."

"Sorry," I say.

"It's not your fault," he tells me. "You don't know how to talk to people. You don't know the things you're supposed to say in these situations. You would say, for example, **I'm sorry for your loss**." There is an edge to his voice.

"I'm sorry for your loss," I repeat.

Llew swerves towards the jetty and walks out to where the rowing boat is moored. I look at it doubtfully.

"Let's go out on the boat. It's a beautiful day," he says.

"It's not safe," I say.

"It is," he tells me, and somehow I find myself climbing in, my shoes darkening with the water already in its gut, and I am reminded that I will do anything he wants.

I let Llew row. The boat doesn't start taking on water at once, but I know it will not be long. The air is close. There is a sharp noise somewhere far above, or in my eardrums, I can't tell, and the sea is too flat. I hold on to the side of the boat until I can't feel my fingertips.

"What are you so scared of?" Llew asks. "I can't fucking relax when you're like this."

"I'm not scared," I tell him.

"I can tell you are. You're so tense. What is it?" he asks. He hits the water with his oar, voice louder. "What is it?"

I can see, too late, the knife in his belt. The rope at the bottom of the boat, snaking around his feet, wet now. My breath comes in shallow bursts, and I know I am dying without him even having to touch me.

Llew stares at me. "You're having a panic attack," he says, with something approaching wonder.

"I'm dying," I tell him.

"No," he says. "You'll be fine." He reaches out and holds my hand, presses his fingers to the base of my palm and I flinch, but all he does is count my pulse aloud until my breathing goes back to normal.

"We'll stop here," he says, laying the oars down.

I will never come further than this from my home, I will never be a person who crosses the border. I will never leave my sisters again. Bargain, or realization, or both. There is dank water around my feet, a tidemark of dirt. And I say a prayer for myself, finally. Prayer for days under the sun. Prayer for sea anemones and perfectly shaped stones and cold water against my hands, and the feeling of being very clean, and movement, explosive movement, the birds wheeling up from the trees, the slates of the roof hot under my skin.

When I look up, Llew is staring at me. It seems incredible that I ever thought his eyes kind. My body has been playing tricks on me all along.

"I need us to go back," I say.

"I'm tired. I don't want to go back yet," he says. He is still looking at me. "Are we too close to the house?" he asks. "Will we be seen?"

We are too close, but I shake my head. He reaches out to me. I unbutton his shirt.

Partway through he pauses, takes hold of the rope, and I know that this is it. Even with my well-trained lungs there is no way I will last more than two minutes in that water with my hands tied, but a great calm comes over me. What I think right at the moment when he ties the knot around my wrists: **It wouldn't be the worst thing in the world.** A life for a life. I have always been ready to give mine for my sisters.

"Trust me," he says. "You'll like it."

I let the grieving man do what he wants. Squeeze my eyes tight shut against the sun, red light fruiting behind my eyelids, and wait.

Joy's echo returning, somewhere, my heart leaping in my chest, because he must still love me really.

Sudden memory of lying down on the recliner in the first days after Mother's disappearance. I am tired; I am looking for my sisters but something about the sun has struck me down. I sleep for a short while in an angular piece of shade. Llew wakes me up by sitting on the end of the recliner and taking hold of my ankle. He is very tender with it. Easy touch, unthinking, then he leaves. I keep that foot so still that I develop pins and needles. Another pathological reaction.

Once he has loosened the rope he dresses quickly and sits back away from me, puts his head in his hands. There is silence for several moments. I debate whether to say the three words I have been carefully considering, whether it will change things.

"That was the last time," he tells me. "Absolutely."

"Why?" I ask.

"Lia," he says. His head sinks lower in his

hands, then snaps up. He looks at me straight. "We can't keep doing this. I told you as much before."

I decide to say the three words anyway, in case they change his mind. I say them very quietly.

He turns around, looks to the house then turns back to me. "I thought you'd be impervious to that sort of thing," he says despairingly. "I thought you might not be like the rest of them." There is something else in his voice too. It takes me a few seconds to understand that it is disgust.

"God," he says, throwing his oar into the bottom of the boat. "I'm grieving, Lia. I'm trying extremely hard to hold it together. Can you give me that, at least? Can you understand not to put anything on me?" His voice is too loud. "What are you expecting?"

To be transformed, nothing more. To know that it is worth it, somewhere in my body, what I have put us through.

"I'm sorry," I say. "But I love you."

He flinches when the words come out of my mouth, and I know that's at least partly why I keep saying them.

"I can't do this now. Not today," he says. "Not ever, if I'm honest. I'm sorry. I wouldn't expect you to understand."

But I do understand. "You're cruel," I tell him. "You're so cruel."

"I don't deny it," he says. "Can you allow it, though? After what I've been through? You have no idea."

My eyes water. I stare at his face, his lips drawn back in a half-grimace, and try hard to hate him.

"Don't cry," he says. "I should be the one crying." Then he is, after all, the back of his hand at his eyes.

"I'm sorry, Lia," he says. "I'm not a good man. Not even at the best of times."

"Why did you do it in the first place?" I ask him.

"Why does anyone," he tells me, not a question. The salt rises off the ocean around us, and I realize that I have heard enough.

"We have to go back," I say, wiping my eyes with the hem of my dress. He turns his wet face away from me. We do not say another word. It is an opportunity, having his back to me, but I don't do anything with it. I cannot hurt him, despite the great pain in my chest, as though I have swallowed air.

At the jetty, we separate without a word. I permit myself a final look at the long shape of him disappearing up the shore, into the house.

I walk down the beach, crying so hard that the horizon doubles, overrunning when it comes to the sky. My pain compels me to fall, but I ignore it. I reach the rock pools, inspect each one in turn to distract myself. Anemones and clams grow vast and ponderous. On the smooth strip of basalt exposed by the tide, going out now, I walk as far as I dare.

On the return, I see something sticking up from the sand, petrified wood or old-world junk. A flag of colour. I go closer, scuffing the sand off with my foot at first, and then kneeling to move it with my hands. Broken planks and fibreglass reveal themselves, painted white and red, the vicious edge of a motor. The sand has drifted deep around them, or they have been there for a long time, or someone must have buried them, I realize, as I pull out more fragments.

I scoop some of the sand back over, stand

up. **You don't have to think about this right now,** I tell myself. And isn't it good, my capability to show kindness to myself finally at this time of need? I walk away without looking back. Later, I will think about it. Not now.

I go to the ballroom and sit there at the piano, pressing note after note, for some time.

Stop being so self-indulgent, I hiss inwardly, when I notice water falling to the keys. I have gutted enough hearts to know they are just orbs of jelly, that even the fish have them.

And then, **I'll sell my soul to you if you can strike his black heart down dead,** I reason half-heartedly with the sea. **I'll be yours for ever if you can just drown him.**

But if he was dead he would never be able to reconsider, to tell me he loved me really, so I take it back with alarm. **Sorry.**

It's just that I am done with love. But there is nowhere else to go.

There are footsteps and I hope they are Llew coming to find me, to tell me that he has made a mistake. I stand up to find it is only Grace.

"Lia," she says, lifting her hands. They are covered in dirt. I blink and look again, the late-afternoon sun through the windows dazzling me. It is blood. It covers the front of her white gown, a deep stain against her chest. **She is hurt,** I think, taking a step towards her. **She is dying.** She says my name again, lowering her hands, and I take another step, and then another.

It's an old story and I'm so tired of telling it—the oldest story in the world and yet I can't put it down, I can't stop it from dragging on my body, so don't make me tell it again. The story doesn't end or even begin with me. You can imagine. You can tell it to yourself.

part three

sisters

grace

I THINK ABOUT the falling woman often. I was on the beach when it happened, so I saw it, although from a distance. How one minute she was in the window. She waved to me, or maybe she was just touching her face, brushing her hair away. All I know for certain is that I did wave back. And then she fell from the window's ledge. There were two other women on the beach with me, and they ran towards her, screaming, even though the scream therapy was on the way out for us. You had decided it was making things worse, not better. We did not want things to be worse.

It was the motion of the falling rather than the trauma of the event that drew me back to the memory. My body was in what felt like perpetual motion in those days. A loop of garden and beach and pool, my hands flexing, standing up to stretch. I could not stay still. Yet that particular gesture, the beauty of it. To fall and then to stop.

In the days afterwards, Lia and I secretly pulled a mattress on to the floor in one of the empty rooms and experimented for hours. We climbed up on to stools and let our bodies go. But our movements were too propulsive. We were too eager.

It was years before I thought to ask you: **What the fuck was all that about?** You told me that I must have been mistaken, that nobody had fallen. Children were prone to drama and invention. Whenever I tried to open a window upstairs, they were painted shut. And you told me, well, yes, they were painted shut to protect the babies, the small and dangerous people hell-bent on dying, on pushing stones down their throats or burying themselves alive. Which is to say, it was all for me.

For maybe a year, I found I could believe the windows had always been shut. That the woman had been a trick of the light. But it was after that day that the women started to be turned away when they reached us. And one day the memory opened up again, despite your efforts, and that time I let it.

My plan was to call my own baby Magnolia, after my favourite tree in the garden. It blooms rarely. For the last two or three years it has been properly dying. The day when we will have to take the chainsaw to it isn't far off.

I would have held my daughter to my chest in a length of swaddling fabric. Strapped her to my back for when the emergency came. For when the tides rose. For when the sky fell.

I keep the gun under my pillow since Mother left, along with my knife. Every morning I touch the metal, familiarize myself with the mechanisms. It is cold and undeniable in my hands. I took it out to the terrace once, an afternoon when everybody else was in the pool below me. With my elbows propped up on the pillows of a recliner, I picked the men off one by one. I put four or five imaginary bullets into Llew's body alone. It helped.

With Lia and Llew gone, James tells us to come with him. We follow him up to the terrace. "Air," he tells us. "We need air." I cannot disagree with that. James lies down on a recliner and puts his hands over his face. He does his ugly man's crying with no regard for us. I am essentially compassionate, so I let him get on with it. On the table next to his body are the binoculars left from the ghost sighting. I notice something out on the sea, a boat. Sweeping the ocean with the lenses, I see the face of my own sister. Llew touches her. He puts his big and dreadful arms around her. There is nothing I can do.

I have no memories of the old world, though you always insisted I did. You spoke of them as a kind of shrapnel—damage lodged in my heart and body that nobody else could see. I never had any interest in remembering really, but you didn't think this important.

You explained to me, one day when we were alone, when Mother was somewhere below, probably taking a nap: you had saved all you could. That is, we had proved ourselves the only ones worth saving.

When the building is burning, you rescue your loved-most. I knew this. But for a father, you explained, it is never so simple.

. . .

James sits up, squints out to sea once he sees me watching.

"Give me those," he orders for the first time, gesturing at the binoculars. I don't want to, but I relinquish them. He looks through them for thirty seconds or so, then lowers them.

"As I suspected," he says. "Well, it's done now. The damage is done."

Sky wants to look too, but he shakes his head. He throws the binoculars on to the floor. The lenses crack, but my sister and I do not flinch. I am interested in his new and proprietary violence. Finally, inevitably, he's showing what he really is, his face crumpling the way yours had started to do in the last days, like the effort of his muscles holding his expression together is unbearable. I watch him very calmly. I am assessing my next move.

He puts his hands on my wrists and looks earnestly down to where his dirty fingernails rest against my veins. I let him do this, though it repulses me.

"I want to tell you some things," he says. "I need to tell someone. I'm sorry that it has to be you, but who else can I tell?"

I invite the confessionals of men. I am not

a stranger to them. Absorbing the guilt and the sorrow is something the world expects of women. This is one of the things you taught me about love. "All right," I tell him, the way I told you.

"Let's go inside," I say. "Let's go to my room. But Sky has to stay here."

He nods. Sky protests, but I still her with a look. I hope she has the sense to hide.

For the last couple of days I have been composing a constant eulogy to our world. **Goodbye, trees. Goodbye, grass, brown and dying. Goodbye, sea and sand. Goodbye, rocks. Goodbye, birds. Goodbye, mice, lizards, insects.** I know, somehow, our time is drawing to a close. The sky above us is burning out. The borders will no longer hold.

With James walking ahead of me, I carry on with my litany. **Goodbye, wallpaper. Goodbye, sweet light of late afternoon. Goodbye, carpet. Goodbye, ceiling and crumbling plaster. Goodbye, doors.**

James moves in a shuffle as if something is causing him a lot of pain, one hand clasped loosely to his chest.

. . .

In my room, he makes his confessions. The dust swirls through the light, and the open windows bring in the smell of the sea. He starts with irrelevancies. He starts with things I already know or have guessed. "I kissed Lia," he tells me after a while. He swallows. "Or she kissed me, but I didn't stop it right away. I wanted to do it."

I do not comment. I fetch him a glass of water for his cracked voice, and when he drains it I walk to the bathroom and fetch him another, meeting my own eyes in the mirror as the water from the tap fills the glass. **Keep him talking,** I tell myself. **Stay away,** I tell my sisters, wherever in the house they might be.

"The world is not what you have been told," he says after the second glass. He is reckless now, as if the water has triggered something in him, strengthened his resolve somehow. He speaks as if from a long way away. "I mean, the world is very terrible, but you have been told a number of things that are untrue."

I ask about the women, with their dying lungs and shrinking skin. I saw the proof of them with my own eyes, swept their hair from the ground, burned bloody handkerchiefs. He shrugs.

"It's not for me to disregard their pain," he says. "They are in the minority. There are mysteries everywhere. Sicknesses wherever you go."

"But you can't deny that men are killing women?" I say.

"Well, no, I can't. But it's not like you think."

So tell me, I think, impatient.

We would be able to go outside, he tells me: the gauze masks that women sometimes wear are only affectations. All of it is smoke and mirrors, overreaction. We would be able to eat the food without it sticking in our gullets, without it radiating bile through our guts. We would not be poisoned by the world, if that's what we are worried about. We could be women like any other, taking the usual precautions. Yes, the risk of violence upon us is higher. Even he as a man can't disregard that! Can't lie to us about it! But also: we could lounge by poolsides there too. And we could meet others. Other women. Men, too. Maybe fall in love, if we wanted to? He says it like that, as a question, almost hopeful.

As if that will be the draw, the sweetening of the deal.

Love was a great educator over the last years, and especially those last months, with you. It taught me first of all that women could be enemies too. Past, present and future. To my own horror I found myself awake late, pacing my room. Had to look away when you kissed Mother, extravagantly, on the cheek at breakfast. My sisters were safe territory, but I still saw them through a vision changed. I saw for the first time that there would be women who took what I wanted, and so I became more protective of myself. I changed alone, spent time in meditation, pushing the gifts you gave to me under the bed, hoarding them so the others would not know.

It also taught me that loss is a thing that builds around you. That what feels like safety is often just absence of current harm, and those two things are not the same.

James is still talking about the life that is open to us. How we could explore vistas of mountain and lake and shore. The countries beyond this limited coast. We could wear shimmering fabrics. Walk in crowds with the evening air hot on our faces, the smell of food and smoke. For the first time James speaks with authority. The world has not been kind to him, I can tell, yet he loves it anyway. It is a man's place. His survival is implicit, a survival taken for granted.

He is more and more animated. "Look, where you are, it is one specific part of the world. There is so much more of it. And not even that far away, either. It would take you a long time to get through the forest. But if you go around the sea, well, it takes no time at all to get out of the bay."

I have always believed our home to be an island. A healing place, untouched, something skipped over and forgotten. A geographical miracle. But it is mainland, like everywhere else. It is just another part of the coarse, toxic earth. You lied to us about this. And so what else?

The shock is physical, reverberating in my fingers, my arms. But James does not notice it. Instead he stops talking, stands up and goes to the window. He becomes calmer, remembering the world like that. He rests his forehead against the glass.

"We made contact," he says as he looks out towards the sea. "We found a way. They're coming."

"And what about us?" I ask. Already I have been thinking about where we can hide. Where we will wait it out while the men prepare themselves to leave. They can take what they want. The silver cutlery, heavy in the palm. Your notes. They can pull Gwil's body from the soil. They can raze the house, for all I care.

"Grace," he says, turning around. "You and your sisters. We're taking you too." He sits on the floor. "King is alive. He is the one who sent us." He looks up at me. "Everything has been for you, all along."

But I didn't ask for any of this, I told myself in the mirror sometimes after the women had all left, and then again after you had disappeared, **I have never fucking asked for this.** I would hold my breath and think about the time I walked through the forest until the border came upon me, how I stepped over the wire without hesitation. My sisters did not know.

You found me very soon. I didn't go far.

Blundering and ill-equipped, a person who had never tried to escape before. The idea had not occurred to me until then. The pits of my footprints swelling with the dismal autumn rain. Hair plastered to my face, my neck and shoulders bare in my nightgown. I thought you might kill me there. I was an admittance of failure. Something about me was changing, was going to a place you could not follow. Yet you were able to lift me in your arms and you carried me back, though I hit at your face, tried to gouge your eyes out. You put me down at that, and tied my hands.

That was how I learned the true meaning of your old mantra, **The love of the family justifies all.**

I cannot breathe for a second. My instincts have failed me. I was so sure I felt you dead, your body no longer transmitting to mine, the ways bodies do when they are in love. The way I could sense you from rooms away. Knew when you were returning to us across the sea. But I was wrong.

James tells me that you warned him we would be afraid. You explained there was a chance we would harm ourselves. It was the way we had been raised, with those small knives at our neck. It was so imperative that we were returned to you unhurt. The men would need to go gently, gently. Win our trust, show their vulnerabilities.

"He wanted you to have the baby away from here," he says. "It would have been a new start."

"But I do not want one," I explain. A new start, I mean.

"They're on their way. They'll be here in hours. It will not be so bad, I promise you. I'll see to that." He puts out his hand to mine, but I don't take it.

Midsummer of the year I ran away, Lia and I had discovered we liked to tan with our tops off in the old greenhouse. It was ripe with oxygen. Smashed pots everywhere. We dragged cushions from our own bedrooms to lie on, and opened up the panels in the glass roof for air. We were closed in but it was our own decision, for once. The glossy leaves of abandoned foliage sheltered our bodies. We had not yet learned that they were shameful.

. . .

Love always asks you to sacrifice something, I know that now. Always demands complicity. I think of Mother over dinner, one evening a long time ago, telling us, "Even if it is a failed utopia, at least we tried."

I didn't understand what she meant. My sisters didn't either. She was drunk, her fringe at a jaunty angle. Earlier that day she had cut it in a rough chunk across her forehead, but we had shied away from the scissors. You had told her she looked ugly and she had cried for a long time. Her eyes were still red.

You knew what she meant, of course. When she said those words you became very still, taking up all the air with your dangerous silence. We froze in position to see what would happen next.

"Go to bed," you told us. We closed the door behind us and listened, hands pressed to the wood. You were talking in a low voice. I heard Mother's rise, then fall.

We went to bed eventually, but not before I heard the start of Mother's crying again. She raised her voice momentarily, enough for me to hear a single phrase. "How long can we go on like this?" she said. "How long?"

The eldest child has to be the toughest,

else she will not escape the mistakes wrought upon her. The body of the eldest child is naturally a weapon. She told me that years later. "So you made mistakes?" I asked. She kept looking at me, her eyes glassy. She knew what I meant. "I am not anybody's weapon but my own," I told her.

"Mother," I say, grasping for any comfort. "Is Mother with them? The people coming for us?"

He just looks at me, his eyes more watery than ever.

"You killed her," I say, not a question. "You killed her." He bows his head.

"It's not like what you think," he says.

It had been Llew, of course.

"King only wants you and your sisters," James says. "You're still young, Grace." He pauses. "Thirty isn't too old to start all over again, not by any means. If that's what you're worried about."

We are your property, your rightful goods. Mother was worn out, a liability; I have replaced her. Half the age, body and mind equipped for survival. It is simple. You would explain it to us so reasonably if you were around. We would see it as the only rational act.

"You still have so many years of your life ahead of you," James said. He looks at me with unbearable pity.

And too many years behind me, I want to tell him. They gather like a bank of water. Like a heavy wave. I cannot forget those years, let them break over me. I will not.

One morning we found the greenhouse splintered, the glass a shimmering blanket around wire frames. You had realized what we were doing and taken a sledgehammer to every pane. You might as well have staved in our hearts.

James goes into more detail. It was Mother's fault, he explained. She humiliated Llew at the start, the strip-search, the denial of water. Better men than him would have nursed that seed of resentment. He could not be blamed, actually. It happened almost by accident. It was a kind of self-defence. He had underestimated his strength, underestimated the pressure of his hands, the heaviness of his swing.

"You can understand that, can't you?" James asks me. "You can understand how that could happen, with someone like him?"

There were men who naturally caused great harm. It is built into them. You had warned us. You are one, though you would never admit it.

James and Llew had closed her eyes and put fishing weights on her body and left her out at sea, alone.

In the distant past I spoke to the damaged women, when I could. I was young. They were reluctant to give me details, instead pressing my palms with secret, useless trinkets. Textured soaps, shells on pieces of twine. I hated these offerings even more than the samplers we stitched with swollen fingers. Everything was so heavy with intention and none of it worked.

What I needed from the women was information. I knew even then that it was important to arm myself. Know your enemy. When you and Mother occasionally told us things about the world it had to be done under controlled conditions, with time for recovery. It wasn't enough.

The more I learned, the more I realized that even being physically removed from it wouldn't save us. The violence came for all women, border or no border. It was already in our blood, in our collective memory. And one day the men would come for us too.

That was the source of the anger. Stronger in the damaged women, but it was also there in us. The potentiality. I still scream in my sleep. So does Lia, though I have never told her. It's not like cruelty has not been wrought upon us.

With every new discovery I found myself looking at you with new eyes, you who had renounced the world, you who claimed to put your love of women above all things. Possibly you were hurting me already, in the name of love. I was not sure at that time how it would manifest in me.

It didn't take long to find out. Pains in my abdomen, the metallic taste in my mouth. I had always slept on my front like a child, but my chest became too painful. I thought I was dying for some time.

. . .

I want to know everything about the men now, for the first and only time. I look at James's sodden red face and want to know his histories, his heartbreaks. The refracting decisions that brought him, them, here. I picture the two brothers tussling in dirt, Gwil's age. I want to discover what turned them into themselves. I want to know how I could become heartless too.

"Tell me how you know King" is all I can say in the end. The puzzle that sent these men from you to us.

It was nothing special. They knew you from decades ago. You inspired terror in your time. If you were a certain kind of man, you could have five hundred lives. You could shake them all off like dead skins.

I expect to learn it was Llew's doing that brought you here, but no. It was James who owed you the favour. Llew had just come along. You had been very gracious about it. He was not keen to see his older brother killed. It was an act of love too. If there is one thing we know, it is acts of love. This does not make me feel better.

. . .

"King considers your life here a failure," James tells me. "King has decided a fresh start is best for all involved."

I do not know what he means. Our lives are our lives.

James is crying again, hopeless, as if realizing that his confessions have not made anything better. Nothing will make him feel better.

"I have told you too much," he says. He grasps for me. I close my eyes for one second.

"We will not go," I tell him. "You don't know what kind of man King is."

"I do," he said. "Oh, believe me, I do. And I'm sorry." He cries too hard to speak for a second. "I am truly sorry for what we've done to you and yours."

Shuffling closer, I put an arm around him. He holds on to me as if drowning. With one hand I touch his back lightly, and with my other I feel under my pillow. My hand moves over the gun, finds the knife. It is so sharp that I have cut my finger before accidentally and barely noticed. As clean as a wound can get. It is the quieter option, the one that feels right. I am surviving, the way you taught me.

His head is still on my shoulder, my dress wet as he sobs. There is a new ruthlessness in me, or maybe it has always been there, waiting for the emergency—maybe you were the one to see it first, were right about us all along. I raise my hand.

It is strange, the things that prepare you. When I put the blade to his neck and press, aiming for just under the ear, dragging down under the jaw, I might have thought about your lifting the chickens by their feet and swiping the knife across their throats. They struggled and you laughed at them, doing it down on the shore so the sea would rinse the blood, take it as a gift. The rest of the birds with feathers patched, gathered in fear.

I might have thought about skinning rabbits. One clean slit from throat to tail. Their wet bodies like the inside of fruit. We stopped eating them because of the high levels of toxins. Rabbits could go beyond the border and return.

Instead, I think about the dark rooms where you tried to save me. Wipe my traumas clean. Your large hands at my head, feeling my skull for memories, for things I shouldn't know. Speculative, planted, real. A wheeled machine made of metal that leaked smoke. A sky with tall buildings crowding up into it. A pale woman fallen on the terrace, her blonde hair meshed over her face.

I think about my sisters, lining up with me and Mother for our annual portrait. You, hefting the box of the camera on to a tripod. You, developing the photo in that tiny bathroom, the light shut out, basin full of chemicals. You, holding me in there sometimes, tightly and too tightly, in the pitch-black. Nobody was to disturb the man at work. I liked it, the too-tightness, though I am not a person used to liking anything. The photo placed ceremoniously in the lounge. No man documented. The man's role is to make the document. The necessary curating of our lives.

I think about being drowned in the pool with Lia, back when we were the same person, split down the middle like the heart of a tree. Sick with dread every night when it started happening. Lia's face in front of mine as we were held down. Lia reaching out to hold my hands, to stop me thrashing. She always coped better. Things were easy then. We belonged to each other. There was no question of what love went where.

One final thought: the three of us in my room, full of water, stomachs distended. Our collective boredom a hum over our bodies. Lia had just started hurting herself in earnest. We were supposed to be grateful.

It is messy. It is very terrible. He reels back from me in horror. It is not like how Mother had told us it would be. Every other death has happened offstage. And now here I am, confronted with the absurdity of it.

I put the gun and the knife in my pocket. Close the curtains, get blood on them. I no longer care. Let the blood get everywhere. I turn my back on the slumped body and sit down on the floor for a long time.

What it was like to be in love with you: fucking awful, even after you revealed it was technically all right. The love of the family magnified. Except I wasn't of your blood. Except you had raised me like your own. Except I knew no other families to compare ours with.

It was like having a permanent hangover.

A pure, lightning nausea, not unlike how it would later feel to be pregnant.

"What am I to my sisters?" I asked you after you told me who I really was, and you said that I was still a sister but only half, that four pints of the blood in my veins was alien. That the differences would probably manifest themselves as my age increased, as the three of us stretched away from each other. I cried to find out that half of my blood was unknowable. Again, a thought that came back to me when I was pregnant: **What is this inside me?**

What it was like to be in love with you: the secret prayer I said in the days after your death, even as I was mourning—genuinely mourning, I promise you, because I am not totally monstrous—

Please stay away
Stay under the sea
Be gone
I'm sorry

You told me to stop calling you **Father,** because you weren't my father, because the parameters had changed, but I don't think I managed it before your death. I kept slipping back into habit. I had been one of three for so long.

There was so much you and Mother kept from us about our own bodies. Let us think them incapable, weak, when nothing could be further from the truth. Kept us only in a twilight health, our bones always painful, our teeth rotting where they lay in our mouths. Vitamin pills the shape and size of thumbnails when I was pregnant. "Deadly for your sisters," Mother intoned darkly. When she turned away I was able to read the back of the packet, which said otherwise.

"You girls are a new and shining kind of woman," you told me, a year before my body changed. Evening this time. My sisters and I had finally grown used to the new rhythms of the house without the damaged women. A soporific truce. You and I were out on the terrace with blankets across our knees. All had been forgiven.

Love was a rising water coming up around me. You were pointing out the stars with your large and damaging hands, explaining what each one meant. Most of them meant **Caution,** or **Be good.** Variations on these.

"There has never been anyone like you in the world," you continued. Your voice was grand.

"Well, I wouldn't know about that, would I?" I said.

The night you explained what was happening to me—your face impassive as usual, but a faint energy coming off you, an excitement—the air had seemed so beautiful and bracing. The forest shielding us. The sea letting sound and light ring out, true as a bell. I had used a stick you brought back from a voyage, floury latex gloves to protect my hands from the modern object. My own bathroom, dark, with everyone else oblivious in the lounge. Two blue lines in a box.

When I had stopped crying, I went to Lia's room and waited for her to come to bed. I didn't want to be alone then. Lia, with her strange eyes illuminated by the moon and no knowledge of what had come before, or what was to come.

. . .

"You will inherit all of this," you told me on another evening on the terrace. "This is where you belong."

We padded silently down through the sleeping house, to the kitchen, where you cut me a slice of the blood sausage that you ate late at night, men's food, forbidden. I chewed it but it became gristle in my mouth. Swallowing was impossible. I spat it into the sink, dry-heaved. You rubbed my back. You held my hands. "See?" you said, softly.

For a short while, just after she discovered you and me, Mother and I went through a phase of becoming closer. I was her daughter first; a granddaughter added to the equation. Slow-moving, not yet showing. We spent a lot of time together. She was not always openly malicious.

We sat together with our sewing, facing each other across the dining table. Occasionally we duelled with hard words, hers worse than mine. My heart wasn't in it. My heart was elsewhere. Occasionally she would crease up her face in the way that was her version of crying, but I did not cry once.

She told me stories about her childhood

that I understood were supposed to be supplication, explanation. Stories I did not want to hear, about eating hot bread with her own mother, about mingling with other children. Boys and girls. They pushed each other to the ground. It was a different time. I asked for a memory about my real father, made bold by the changes in myself, but she refused. She kept it from me because she could.

I did not want her to be a fellow woman. Sometimes she was my enemy and sometimes she was just my mother, an enemy in a different way.

Mother must have felt the fact of your aliveness like a shame, a wound. She wrote you letters—not that she had any way of sending them. I found them on the first day of her absence. I went straight to her room, alone, to see what I could find. What I could strip or use or hold between my hands and guess the meaning of. The gun. A lipstick, frosted orange, not her colour. Not anybody's colour, I found, once I smeared it across my mouth.

I thought the letters were elaborate metaphor. Her grief failing to comprehend that you were a piece of meat by then. My heart softened. There had been romance in her, after all.

Each one ended with **Do not send for the girls,** or some sort of plea built upon this. I took this as her invocation against our deaths, Mother writing those words down as a prayer to the sea. A message for you to pass on, wherever you lurked, the other ghosts a shoal around you.

I'm sorry I made you leave, said another one, but I hadn't read too much into that at the time. I knew survivor's guilt when I saw it.

The first time I hit you, you laughed. My nails took off a small amount of the skin on your cheek. There was no blood.

"You're like your mother," you told me. "Vicious."

You were right, she was vicious. Left her fingernails to grow long, filed them to a point and painted them in too-bright colours. She had been behind the more sadistic therapies. Whether she truly believed in being cruel to be kind, or whether she just secretly hated us, I cannot quite decide.

For a while I thought she might have poisoned you and dragged your body out to the forest somehow. Her tears were fake, an empty gesture. The others were taken in by them when you had gone.

Through it all, she told us she loved us so often that it became its own violence, something it was impossible to turn down.

And every day, the border of the world drawing closer to us. And every day having to look into Mother's face and pray for her health, for her heart, despite everything that had been done to us. And done to her.

Somehow, downstairs. Walking towards the sound of music, into the ballroom, a person playing badly. Lia. She watches me for a second across the piano, then stands up. I call her name, once, twice.

"What have they done to you?" she asks. She is shaking. I look down at myself, the blood staining my dress and forearms, and find that I can't speak.

We find Sky in the kitchen, foraging in a cupboard, her body half-concealed. Lia and I put our hands upon her. Together we move as one up to Lia's room.

The emergency flares in our limbs. Blood

pulsing. My extremities cold. James could have contaminated me. Who knows what disease the men truly carry. Who knows what Lia now glows with inside her bones. The blood is hardening on my dress already. In the dark of the corridor, my sisters swallow the news without question, not even a **why.**

You blamed my early exposure to the outside world for why I never grew tall like the other sisters, remained small like Mother. It was also why I sometimes had attacks of breathlessness as a child. A squeezing in my chest, a vestigial sense of doom. These have improved as I've aged. You were satisfied with how well your therapies had worked.

I watch my sisters move now. They walk in front of me, feet stumbling as they process the new information, what it will mean for us. Fear makes me cough. If we stop moving it will gather in our joints, I know. It will fill our lungs, and we will seize up or die.

When we reach Lia's room I watch as my sisters take it in turns to vomit into the en suite's toilet, neatly, to get some of it out. Fingers down the throat. I wash my hands in the sink once they're done, the blood pinkening the water. A smear of it near my mouth that I wipe off with a damp tissue.

"Llew will find out what I've done," I tell them when I return to the bedroom. My sisters sit on my bed, vigilant and pale. "We need to decide what to do."

We could kill him and keep ourselves safe.
We could leave immediately, let Llew find James's body, hope that we would be long gone.
We could walk into the ocean with our hands linked and know it was over, that it was finally over and would always be over.
We could beg for Llew's forgiveness, beg him to protect us from you.
We could wound him grievously to keep him loyal.
We could pretend it was nothing to do with us.
We could forgive him.

I take Lia's hands as we list the options. It has been a long time since I have touched her for more than a second. They are thinner than I remember, her temperature low.

"He will never forgive us," I say, as gently as I can.

There is silence. Lia puts her fingers in her mouth and chews at the cuticles. When she puts her hands into her lap they are bleeding quite a lot. She looks at them in surprise and goes to the bathroom to rinse them under the taps again.

"We have to kill him," I tell Sky while Lia is out of the room. A deep weariness comes across me. She stares at me, but nods. I place my weapons on the bedspread between us. I am afraid of her suddenly, of how accepting she is of this. At what it reveals about the life that we have lived. Maybe it is just that she is no longer the baby. Maybe she is perfectly equipped for the world, the way you planned all along.

When Lia comes out, we put our arms around her.

"No," she tells us. "No, no, no." She tries to push us away. "We can't."

"It's the only way," I tell her.

"I love him," she says, uselessly.

"We can't do it without you," I say.

. . .

I watched Lia with the men from the window, the day I first realized something was happening between her and Llew. She lay barely clothed between them, light glinting dangerously off the pool by their feet. They let the toxic words fall out of their mouths with no care for what they could do to her. At the time I had thought, **Sister, have you no initiative?** Sit underneath the parasol, at least. Could she not submerge herself in the water? Could she not have kept some distance? It made my hands shake to watch them. The inexcusable lack of caution.

Always watching and waiting, when it came to my sister. Half of my blood. Even before I knew this, I sometimes felt closer to the damaged women than to my own family. My feet had walked on their land. I worried I was beyond saving. I worried it would not take much to tip me over the line.

I thought of Lia and Llew standing among the trees, face to face, or lying down in any place they could find, and I was jealous, not because of him, but because of what it felt like to be seen. To be known. So I closed my eyes and lived through her for a second, tried to spark up the dormant connection of our minds with something approaching guilt.

Thumb to the cheekbone. Palm cupping the ear. The birds, their jittery song. Cicadas, the background thrum of the sea, oppressive heat. Llew is quiet. He understands that seduction has to happen if he is going to get her to risk her life. That the light has to touch down in the right place. The heart must be willing. The heart must be a traitor.

But we are all traitors in some way. Once Llew was sitting next to me and he put a hand on my knee when nobody else was in the room. I lifted it up at once and he replaced it. It wasn't funny. I lifted up his hand again and scratched him, hard. And he was shocked. His eyes, narrowing, told me he wasn't a person used to failing.

I stuck closer to Sky than usual after that, surprised her with my attentions. I thought I saw him appraise her once, a quick consideration—eyes from head to toes. That was enough for me. Yet when I told her not to be alone with him, she looked horrified at the very idea. Lia was the only one who was not afraid. Or more accurately, she was a person made brave, made desperate, by necessity, and finally I can understand this.

I can see how it went. What else was there for me to do besides observe, watch my sisters as they changed around me? Llew keeping close to Lia, trailing her movements in the dim evening light, through windows as we stretched. The reaction started with his arrival. It was inevitable, unstoppable.

Then the boredom. I could sense it radiating off him as the heat built, in the insolence of his body as he lay by the pool. He pulled away from her. He stopped his looking. Lia had proved a disappointment. She was just like every other woman. Eager and tender-hearted. That knot of grief in her chest begging to be undone.

It is not a crime, to lose interest. Perhaps even he did not recognize the particular cruelty of his actions.

The anger of the women seemed a force from outside them. It was an anger that welled up deep in their chests. Without it, they would not have been able to survive. I personally have always welcomed it. The moments of power. The burning in my stomach.

Be angry, I wanted to tell Lia. She moved around the house in an underwater trance. I recognized it too well. She couldn't see that I was trying to protect her. She couldn't see that Llew was nowhere near perfect, that he was just slippery-eyed and opportunistic. In her strangeness, she deserved far more than the ordinary. Even I, knowing nothing about anything, knew he was ordinary. Knew he should be trembling in front of her. **Don't be grateful! Be angry! Be tough!** I knew she was capable of it. It made his reduction of her all the worse. To see my sister like that, weak, when in many ways she is the strongest of the three of us.

I still remember the love therapy when I was ordered to hold a flaming candle against my palm for as long as I could. But the smell of the melting wax terrified me. I was not used to feeling or showing terror. I remember you and Mother looking at each other as I cried and trembled, as if you had isolated something.

Lia took the candle instead. That year, she was my loved-most, and I was hers. The irons had aligned. Double the love. Double the luck. She hesitated only a little before moving her other hand to the flame. We all watched as the fire licked at her skin and the wind moved the sand over our bare feet. **One thousand and one. One thousand and two. One thousand and three.**

There was a small charred hole in her palm for the next month. It wept yellow water and Mother washed it with antiseptic twice a day. Lia didn't cry once.

There is much I owe my sister.

Lia and I are the only ones to go downstairs, looking for Llew. We insist Sky stays behind. The gun is too heavy in my hand. There is no sound or sign of him. He could be hiding already, could have sensed the change in the atmosphere. Lia shakes next to me. There is no way to make this easy for her.

In the dining room, I rest the gun on a white-clothed table and flex my hands. We move to the doors to search for his shape on the water, on the beach. Between the kitchen, reception, the dining room, the ballroom, there are too many doors into this house, more than we could cover even if Sky were here too. **Think,** I tell myself. **Think**.

"Maybe he's in the pool," Lia suggests.

"No," we hear a male voice behind us say, and of course we turn to find Llew holding the gun in his hand, eyes on us.

Maybe he did tremble in front of her, in private, when there was nobody to see, nobody to pretend for. I cannot pass judgements on the love of other people. I have done a lot of wrong.

Long afternoons in her room. My sister's wide, unpretty smile. I only imagined them to see if I could visualize harm being done to her. And I tried to recall how Llew went around afterwards. Whether he walked like someone falling in love. Because you did. Your steps slowed. Your eyes became heavy, you became forgetful. That's when I knew we were in trouble, a trouble deeper than I could have dreamed of.

"Are you going to explain why you're carrying this around?" Llew asks. He is smiling. He is a fucking piece of work.

"Just in case," I say. I meet his eyes. I want to spit on the ground in front of him.

"Right," he says. "Where's James? I can't find him anywhere."

We are silent.

"Where's James, girls?" he asks again, much louder, no longer smiling, and I am sick of him—I am sick of the men, of how they reduce us, how even now I am cowering.

Lia and I move closer to each other. I want our bodies to be doubled so we can strike him down. His own body moves a step closer to us, then another, and his hands on the gun are practised, steady, and in that steadiness I can see the appeal of him for the first time, I cannot blame Lia entirely for what she has done.

Refrain of the man, universal: **This is not my fault!**

See also: **I absolve myself of responsibility.**

And: **I never said that. You can't take the actions of my body as words.**

It is Sky who saves us. It will always be a woman who saves us, we know that now. The protections of men are only ever flimsy and self-serving. She followed us after all and she sees what Llew is going to do and she lifts the vase high over her head. We do not see her until he has crumpled.

The images are like flashes of light. The shift. His face slackening, the thud of the vase where it falls to the floor and cracks, but does not shatter. It is good to see him on the ground where he belongs. We breathe, recover ourselves. We do not think about what almost happened. Sky finds twine in the kitchen and we tie him up, ankle to ankle, wrist to wrist. He remains unconscious as we drag him out of the house and down to the shore. Sand catches in his clothes, his hair. There is something rising in us, and I am glad. I want to stop for a moment and let it wash over me.

The protocol in this instance is the lifeguarding that we have been taught. A subservience, a kindness. An acknowledgement that during times of violence, it is always worse for the women.

"If men come to you, show yourself some mercy," you said. "Don't stick around and wait for them to put you out of your misery."

But now here is Llew, powerless on the

sand. Our parents have revealed themselves as fallible already. I am loath, when we have come so far, to draw a knife across my own throat.

A new kind of life-guarding, then, a ritual that we own. Neutralization of his body, its power. A reclaiming of our shores. Suddenly things become very clear to me.

His eyes open and he fixes them upon me, but though I return his stare I do not address him.

Instead I half-turn to Lia, keeping my gaze on the man at my feet. "Fetch the salt."

The most surprising thing love taught me was that I wouldn't do anything differently, despite it all. I would not have said **no** to you. I would not have turned away early mornings of light, the smell of ozone and rain through the window. I would not have given away the days, alone, of me and the baby. Kicks against my lungs and liver. The baby said **Stay alive** more compellingly than anything I have ever known.

Sudden love, when gifted to a habitually unloved person, can induce nausea. It can become a thing you would claw and debase yourself for. It is necessary to wean yourself on to it, small portions. I doubt very much Lia has been doing so.

I stare at Llew, writhing against the sand, as we wait. I hope he can read my thoughts. They say: **Llew, I knew someone like you. I know you think we are nothing. I know you come from a world where we would already be dead. I know you are a man who wants to kill women, because that is every man, even the ones who claim to love us. But your body will not save you here. You are no longer in your territory. This belongs to us. It always will**.

We sisters have always been cruel in our own way, but I believe our cruelty is allowable. It kept us alive, it helps us to put things right. It has been helpful to look at it as a margin of error, morality-wise.

We throw the salt upon him, handful upon handful, and he makes little reaction, blinking under our actions. It stills him; he is baffled. Then we move in and we start to kick at him. It feels good to hurt him finally, his solid and implacable body. But it is not long before I hand the gun to my sister.

"You're the one who has to do it," I tell Lia.

She takes the weapon and looks at it with trepidation. Llew watches her, breathing fast.

"You'll be one of us again," I tell her. It is a low blow, and it is the truth.

The last act of love I will demand from her. I know that if she cannot do this, she is lost to us for ever.

Llew's final crime was unforgivable, and I wonder if he felt that in himself. I am being charitable here by assuming that killing would change him. I am imagining him opening his eyes afterwards and seeing us as if for the first time.

Maybe it was guilt that distanced him. Waves of it waking him in the early morning, the remembrance of the thing he had done.

I imagine our home becoming too real to him. No longer a holiday from his life. No longer pool and shore and salt and my sister, suntanned and uncomplicated in afternoon rooms. Just a house falling apart. No paradise.

The ceilings stained with water. Dust gathering on shelves, in corners. Three women moving around it, lost, where once there had been four. Having done that was not power. It was not fun. It had never been fun.

Lia is trembling. She stares at him and her eyes are very large, as if there might be something else she can see in him if she looks close enough. It is hard to stay away from the things that could be the end of who you are, I know.

It comes back to me now. The first time we saw the men. The three of them on the sand, opening up the world. Dirt imprinted on their skin. Strangeness after strangeness. Squinting towards the light, towards our faces. Could it have gone any other way? **No,** I think, watching them together on the sand. How he cringes from her, there. One way only. Us or them.

We feel our mother's absence in ourselves, there on the beach. Suddenly the violence of her loss is pathological. It throws our own disposability into relief. Llew's hands around her throat are also your hands. They are the hands of every man.

. . .

The falling woman was not the first death. I do not know if my sisters remember the woman who never raised her head from the basin. Mother's hands at the back of her neck until it was too late, the small, frantic movements dying away, the damaged women standing up from their chairs one by one. It was not Mother's fault, you explained to everyone, once you had regained control over the room. The woman had not been ready to take the cure. Her body proved unfit. It was her own fault.

We were told we would never receive the water cure ourselves. Our bodies didn't need it. I realized much later that this also meant we would never leave.

Long before the days of the cure, you came for our books. Lia and I had learned to read with them: intelligible romances, comedies, thicker books with blocks of print. Lia was reading too swiftly, enjoying it too much. Fine electricity webbing my sister's brain. The quickness of her sentences gave you pause. You left only the recipe books, lined up on a shelf, their images like living things. Sky never really learned to read, thanks to your actions. Meanwhile, Lia and I taught each other **bouillabaisse** and **sous-vide** and **truss** so that we would not forget. In the absence of red meat, our lips swallowed words. We were eating a lot of peanut butter, jarred dulce de leche. Foods energy-dense and blameless.

Then you came for our hair. Mother kept it cut just beneath our shoulders, lining us up in the ballroom when the season changed and shearing the ends. Mine was the thickest. It curled underneath but not on top. The damaged women were stealing the hair, going through our bins. They were doing it for their own protection, but you put a stop to all that. We could not cut it or give it away to anyone. It tangled around our waists within what felt like months. I used to wake up and think it was down my throat, a hand or a snake, killing me.

Finally you came for our hearts, which had started to vibrate in our bodies like red and pulsing lights. They panicked you. You knew they were signals beaming outwards. You knew they would be the death of us.

I would lie on my stomach for hours, waiting for my feelings to scorch the ground beneath me. You thought we were in need of more drastic therapies. Stricter ways of measuring our loves.

So we portioned it out in finite acts. A kiss to the cheek was worth **this** much. I could hardly spare a hand placed to the small of the back, a slow glance, a smile. Languorous with it. Spiteful. I would give it all away if I could go back. I would touch my sister until her limbs grew black and blue.

When I went into Mother's room just before Gwil's death, I saw that somebody had taken the irons down. All I felt was relief. Finally, finally, there was nothing to tie me to you. Not even my blood, which I didn't have to look at or acknowledge anyway. I could just leave it to do the dirty work in my body.

"Can you tell me why you don't love me?" Lia asks him, very quietly.

"I do," he says, eyes watering. "I do."

"No, you don't," she says. "But I'm interested to know why not."

"Please," he says.

She pauses. "You really hurt us," she says.

. . .

I am so weary of the small and large deaths of my heart.

Despite myself, memories of you that knock me over: small tendernesses. Both my hands held in yours. Gift after pointless gift. A hairband. A china swan, palm-sized. White chocolate that coated the inside of my mouth. Relics.

First time, in the dark light of the study. Nobody would come in. Cot bed in the corner where you slept, alone, during times of great productivity. I was drunk on sharp white wine, and nervy. So were you. A long time coming. Looks and words, your presence in the corner and at the doorway.

Only harm can come of this, I thought afterwards, staring at my face in the mirror of my bathroom. The elation felt dangerous. A bright and skittering ripple inside my stomach, my ribs. It made my hands shake so hard that I could not brush my hair, the hundred ritual strokes each night that Mother had taught us. I had to sit down on the floor. Then I had to lie down against the cold tiling, supine, as if love were a force like gravity. A thing to keep me close and crawling on the ground. **I am going to do myself great harm.**

In these last days, I found a blood-sodden nightgown at the back of Lia's drawer. It looked and smelled like something evil dug up from the ground. At first I didn't know why she had hidden it there. Then I thought about how pale she has been recently, and about the rings around her eyes, and with a deep sorrow I thought, **Not you,** but there was no surprise in it, I had known it was coming.

Maybe the men had been drawn to her from a long way away. Maybe her own body had signalled them to the shore, a haze of light in the air above our home, and they had lifted their heads and howled at the sky with joy to think of us, the girls, helpless under their hands, before they had even seen our faces.

Lia presses her face close to Llew's, but I cannot be sure if she is praying or talking. I can no longer look at her, at them. My face is wet, suddenly.

I feel we should go away and lie down for a long time, somewhere with the smell of ferns, bodies of calm water. I see it, somewhere, a far way off.

I hope, if by any chance you learn of this, it leaves the worst possible taste in your mouth. My sisters are still of you. It has always been that we are what you made us, and so our survival is a tacit endorsement of you, however much we might hate that. But our lives are our lives.

I take Sky's hand and we turn away, walk towards the house, pausing at the edge of the beach. We sit on the wet sand and watch as each wave rushes towards our feet. On the horizon, flat light falls behind cloud.

We wait for the gunshot. It comes soon. Then another. The heat amplifies the sound. Another. Our hearts. Sky puts her hands over her ears. I listen to it all.

I would still like to know your intentions. I would like to have the moment with you that Lia had with Llew, that second before I looked away where I saw him say something into her ear, last words. But then isn't that always like a woman, to want to drag every word and sentiment over and over through the wringer, until the meaning is gone. To over-process. To be absolutely sure.

But do not follow us. Do not look for us. Do not dredge the undergrowth and the shallows, send the birds and the snakes rising from their homes with the rhythm of your feet. Do not press your ear to the ground. Do not cast messages.

The house will fall. The hair in our brushes will turn to dust, our clothes to mould. The only proof of us will be the photographs you took, the places where we crop up in your notes as impossible women, invented into being. These, too, will not last.

It used to bother me that we would leave little trace, but now I have never been more glad about anything. I will wake up in the empty mornings with the absence of you, and I will think, **Glad, glad, glad,** and it will ring like a bell.

Lia comes and sits down next to us. There is blood on her too, but only a little.

"Don't look back at him," she tells us, so

we don't. Precautions against further damage. Too little, too late. My eyes remain trained on the sky. No birds are singing. The air is perfect, finally. There is blood under my fingernails. I will have to fix that.

grace, lia, sky

ONCE THERE WAS a father who thought he could protect us. But that father was not immune to all that the world demanded. We understood it would be difficult, hurtful, to recognize that the danger was in ourselves. That the safe place had been contaminated from the start.

After we wash the last blood from our bodies in Grace's bathroom—the three of us in the tub together, shaking, cupping the water to our limbs and hair—we dress in Lia's clothes. They fit us well enough. White, for the reflective properties. We consider ripping King's suit into pieces, talismans to get us past the border. In the end, we want nothing that has belonged to a man. But another idea occurs to us.

We do not use the curing basin or the ballroom. Instead we return to Grace's bathroom and fill the bathtub almost to the top, salt held in three pairs of hands, sprinkled on the surface in slow, circular motions. It falls to the bottom, twists and dissolves. We perform the water cure for the first time on each other, the only time, the way we have seen it done. We prepare for what is next the only way we know how.

Sky goes first. She kneels of her own volition at the side of the tub. She has never practised for it, but we do what we have to under the circumstances. We are gentle with each other. We let her rise, gasping from the water, without pushing it too much.

Next, Grace. Two hands on the seabird's curve of her neck, Lia's right hand and Sky's left. We hold her down for slightly longer. She lets us, does not move. When she rises up from the water she feels a little faint. She admits it to us. We discuss it among ourselves, take it as a good sign.

Lia goes last. We hold her under for the

longest time. Her time in the swimming pool has trained her well. The ceremony binds us, our blood running to the same tune. We have never wanted to feel Lia's pain, but holding her under the water now, the memory of it in our mouths and eyes, the salt-sting, we let go of that selfishness. When Lia rises, she is smiling. "It was all right," she says to us. "It wasn't as hard as I imagined."

"Goodbye to all of this," we say out loud as we move from room to room. Our home has not kept us safe, in the end. But it has taught us love.

On the shore, we look out to the sea. Goodbye to the ghosts. There are none swimming towards us. Goodbye to the white paint of the house, designed for reflection, for it has failed us.

Our eyes avoid Llew, lying in the same place we left him. He is our message to anyone else who might come to these shores. The message is **This is no place.** The message is **Fuck you.** We hope they will see him and tell others of the dangerous women who discovered a way to save themselves.

The new and shining women. Love slicks us from head to toe. The marks are imprinted on our bodies. We cannot lay down all of that. We wouldn't want to, despite the ways we have been changed. Love still glows at the centre of our being.

Somewhere near the sea's border, the edge of our vision, approaching boats. Large and white. In the air above us, a change. It is time to go.

We move through the garden, past bushes bowed with the weight of their flowers, past thorns and overgrown greenery. By the time we reach the forest, the first dark boughs shielding us from the sun, strange birds are overhead. They fly low. Lia looks up at them.

"I've seen them before," she says. "But never so close."

Keep walking, we tell ourselves. **Keep walking.**

We leave behind our clothes, our weapons, our loved things. We do not even take canteens to hold our water. All the objects stay behind, and we rejoice.

It is possible there are no safe places left. It is possible that we can create a new one with our rage and our love, that other women are already out there, doing the work. We are going to meet them. They will recognize us, no longer children, and hold out their arms to us. They will say, **What took you so long?**

Onwards and onwards, our weary feet. The sound of the birds grows, as if they are swooping lower, as if they are circling. But we are deep in the forest by now. Close to the border.

We watch for snakes. We watch for animals. Gnats or mosquitoes swarm around us and we barely notice. A new noise joins the ones above, a different type of bird with a droning call, but somehow we are still not afraid.

At the border, the rusted barbs of wire, we weigh them down with branches until we can step over. It takes us some time, but we clear them. We stand for a second on the other side of the territory, breathing in the new air. Somewhere in the distance there are voices, but they seem very far away. We look back towards the house, but it is long gone. All we can see is the forest. The cool leaves, the branches.

It is fine. We are fine. We jump on to a felled tree trunk. We wrap our arms around each other. Without noticing it, touch has become easy again. We put our hands everywhere.

There is far to go, and so we do not stop for long. We push the branches with our hands, and beyond each branch is another step for us to take, even as the sound of the birds and the voices grow louder, even as we move further away, even as the leaves cut out the sunlight, and that is its own miracle. The three of us, taking step after step. Our own world somewhere past it, should we walk far enough. We move into it with no fear.

acknowledgements

Many brilliant people have helped bring this book into being. First off a huge thank-you to Harriet Moore, my agent and friend. I am so grateful for your support and faith in me. Thank you to my editors Hermione, Margo and Deborah; I loved working with our fierce international coven. A big thank-you also to Hannah, Simon, Grainne and everyone else at Hamish Hamilton UK/Canada, Doubleday and David Higham Associates. I couldn't ask for a better team behind my book.

I am also particularly grateful for the support from everyone at the **White Review,** and from the team behind the **Stylist** and Virago short-story competition; it was wonderful to finish the edits for my novel in the calm surroundings of The Hurst. I'm thankful too for my former colleagues at Team VSU, who have always been enthusiastic and encouraging about my work.

Many amazing women gave me the courage and motivation to write this book. I would like particularly to thank Lauren Marie Smith, and the dynamic duo that is Krista Williams and Sophie Thomas, for guidance, friendship and wine when needed.

A special thank-you to my parents for their love and belief in me over the years. Thank you to Annys and to Beverley, to whom this book is dedicated. And thank you finally to Christopher, for everything.

About the Author

Sophie Mackintosh won the 2016 White Review Short-Story Prize and the 2016 Virago/**Stylist** short-story competition, and has been published in **Granta** magazine and **Tank** magazine, among others. **The Water Cure** is her first novel.